HURRICANE FORCE

MALCOLM ROSE
HURRICANE FORCE

SIMON AND SCHUSTER

Acknowledgements: Extract from *Earth Shock* by Andrew Robinson ©
1993 and 2002 Thames & Hudson Ltd, London. Reprinted by kind
permission of Thames & Hudson Ltd. Extract from *The Weather Factor* by
Erik Durschmied © 2000 Hodder & Stoughton Ltd. Reproduced by kind
permission of Hodder & Stoughton Ltd.

SIMON AND SCHUSTER

First published in Great Britain by Simon & Schuster UK Ltd, 2005
A Viacom company

1 3 5 7 9 10 8 6 4 2

Simon & Schuster UK Ltd
Africa House
64-78 Kingsway
London WC2B 6AH

A CIP catalogue record for this book is available from the British Library

ISBN 0-689-87284-4

Typeset by M Rules
Printed and bound in Great Britain by
Cox & Wyman Ltd, Reading, Berks

For readers in Angus and Lancashire,
who have given me great encouragement.

PROLOGUE

"There are roughly 2,000 thunderstorms in progress over the Earth at any moment. Together, they generate a million million watts of lightning power – more than the combined output of all the electric power generators in the United States. One storm alone can release well over 500 million litres of water and enough heat to power the US for 20 minutes. A full-blown hurricane, 500 to 1,000 miles or more across and with winds up to 200 mph, contains 12,000 times the water and heat: enough power for half a year. Storms can even affect the fate of nations. In 1588 the Spanish Armada was smashed by storms on the shores of the British Isles; in 1281 a typhoon in Japan left the invading forces of Kublai Khan, the Mongol emperor, at the mercy of samurai warriors, who gave thanks to Kamikaze – the Divine Wind – for the deliverance of their islands."
Andrew Robinson, in *Earth Shock*, Thames and Hudson, 1993

"People have always wanted to be able to do something about the weather. In 1957, the president's advisory committee on weather control explicitly recognized the military potential of weather-modification, warning in their report that it could become a more important weapon than the atom bomb . . . Appropriate application of weather-modification can provide battlespace dominance to a degree never before imagined. In the future, such operations will enhance air and space superiority and provide new options for battlespace shaping and battlespace awareness. 'The technology is there, waiting for us to pull it all together'; in 2025 we can 'Own the Weather'."

A research paper presented to the US Air Force in 1996, entitled *Weather as a Force Multiplier: Owning the Weather in 2025*

"General Eisenhower took a serious gamble when he ordered the invasion of Normandy, based entirely on an educated guess by his chief meteorologist. In the future, military planners will no longer be limited by existing weather patterns. They will be able to design the weather pattern they would like to have or wish to fall on their enemy. They will order up a storm, their technicians will turn on the rain tap and thus create an artificial mud barrier to stop the enemy's armoured columns. They will call up snowfalls, then induce a sudden hot spell to melt the piled-up snow, and flood an entire region. They will destroy harvests

with hailstorms, starve an enemy into submission by droughts, or burn down his forests with man-made thunderbolts."
Erik Durschmied, in *The Weather Factor*, Hodder and Stoughton, 2000

CHAPTER 1

Craig Patmore stared out of his Land Rover's windscreen. A bale of hay, pushed by the strong wind, toppled from the stack in the field, rolled through the open gate, across the track in front of him and plunged down the hill. Gathering more momentum, it headed into the valley, partly rolling, partly bouncing, partly falling. A few moments later, a second bundle charged after the first. The bales were large and round, wrapped in shiny black plastic. It usually took a tractor to shift them, but this storm treated them like gigantic soft toys. A third one took off, following the other two down the slope.

The farmer would be furious. And Craig's computer model was predicting that the wind was merely tuning up for the big event. That was why he'd come to Green Moor. Perched on top of Hunshelf Bank, the tiny Yorkshire community would feel the full force of the gale. It was an ideal location for taking measurements at the heart of the unruly storm. Craig nudged the door open and at once the vicious airstream whipped it out of his hand. For a moment, he thought that the wind would tear it off its hinges. He got out of his Land Rover and immediately the hood of his coat flew up over his head. He had to use both arms to push the door shut.

Another hay bale rolled across the rutted track. A chimney pot clattered down the roof of Windy Bank Hall and shattered when it hit the ground. Craig could see no sign of farm animals – they'd been shut inside for their own safety – but the air carried their pungent smell to his nose.

Tomorrow, the local press would promote this storm to the big league, no doubt calling it a hurricane to make the headlines. Technically, it was a gale-force storm. Right now, the sustained wind speed was perhaps 65 miles per hour, gusting up to about 80 mph. As the centre of the depression approached, Craig expected the wind to exceed hurricane force. Within the next hour, it might even gust to 120 mph. If his computer's calculations were right, hay bales would not be the only victims.

He leaned into the wind, put one hand on the mud-splattered Land Rover to steady himself, and battled his way to the back. He lifted out a portable weather station, which was about the size of a small suitcase on its own stand. Straight away the three cups of the wind monitor began to fly around the spindle like a crazed miniature merry-go-round. The anemometer's software would work out the exact wind speed from the dizzying rate of the cups' rotation.

Craig heaved the weather station over to the side of the track and planted it on its tripod so that the anemometer was exposed to the teeth of the wind. He clung on to the instrument until he'd gone round the three legs and anchored each one with a tent peg. If he had opted for a sheltered position, the device would have been more secure but he would not have got a true reading.

To his left, there was nothing but the steep grassy drop down to the main road through the valley, the steelworks, and the town of Stocksbridge, just north of Sheffield. If the gale blew the weather station over, it would probably not stop until it landed in a mangled heap on the road to Manchester. The bank was dotted with a few rocks but no trees or bushes grew there. On the other side of the rough track, there was only the farmer's field. The onrushing wind would meet no obstacles. Further along the track were the buildings of Hill Top Farm and a row of electricity pylons. Beside him, there was a collection of four masts, transmitting television, radio and telephone signals.

Craig brushed his hand over his tangled hair to try to keep it under control and out of his eyes. The roar of the wind was nearly deafening. A corrugated panel from the roof of a barn flapped upwards and then peeled off altogether. It caught the wind and sailed out over the valley at speed. Watching it, Craig knew that he was at risk. If a sheet like that hit him, it could knock him out, break a bone, or worse. He fought his way back to the Land Rover and dived inside.

While the wind whistled under and over the four-wheel drive, Craig jammed his laptop between his midriff and the steering wheel. He turned it on and, while he waited for it to boot up, he saw an empty flowerpot hurtle past the windscreen like a cannonball. It was pursued by a crisp packet, probably picked up from the village pub. Craig tapped a few keys to open the radio link between the laptop and the temporary weather station. He was interested most in the pressure and wind speed. Already low, the barometer reading was still plummeting. As the atmosphere thinned over South Yorkshire, air rushed towards it in an attempt to fill the vacuum. The more the depression deepened, the wilder the wind would blow. And if Craig's massive computer system at work had modelled the conditions correctly, he would not be far away from the lowest pressure ever recorded in Britain.

The gale was averaging 71 miles per hour now but, before his eyes, the anemometer registered a brief gust of 92 mph. Craig smiled. Exactly what he'd expected. The storm might be putting him in danger but it was vindicating his programming beautifully. Mesmerised by the readings, he sat with his eyes fixed on the laptop monitor as the pressure reading plunged and the wind speed soared.

Outside, the air howled with rage, its din covering

up the creak of metal under stress. In the farmyard, a battered grain silo bent over like an arthritic giant trying to touch its toes. On the main building, two large slate tiles came adrift, scuttled down the roof and disintegrated on the paving stones below.

Craig raised his arms and cheered as the average wind speed burst through the magic 74 mph barrier. If this storm had drawn its first breath and grown over the Atlantic, it would now be a fully-fledged hurricane and it would be received into the world with an official name. Hurricane Craig. If it had been born over the northwest Pacific, it would have been called a typhoon. Typhoon Craig. But this was England and it was a gale-force storm. It would not be given a name.

The anemometer recorded a momentary blast of air at 107 mph and then keeled over, bringing Craig's celebration to an abrupt end. Luckily, the weather station didn't disappear over the edge. One leg of its tripod clung doggedly to the earth.

Right away, Craig got out of the vehicle. He needed the weather station back in action as soon as possible. First, he clung to the door and then, stooping to make himself a smaller target for the wind, he staggered towards the prone instrument. Trying to resist being pushed over, he planted his boot firmly on the ground every time he took a step. The pressure of the wind gave him an instant ache in his chilled ears and head, as if he'd dived deep underwater. It also stung his eyes.

On the footpath behind him, between his Land Rover and Windy Bank Hall, a greenhouse exploded. An unstoppable gust powered through its open door and smashed three flimsy panes, sending pieces of glass flying.

Craig grabbed hold of the tripod's legs that were poking up into the air. The weather station wasn't heavy but pulling it upright felt like reeling in a big fish. Once he'd got the weather station back into position, he squatted down and, using a stone, hammered the pegs through its feet and into the muddy earth.

Beyond the farm buildings, an electricity pylon let out a groan so loud that it was audible above the screaming wind. Buckling, the metal monster wavered for a few seconds, held in place by its seven heavy cables. Then, one by one, the power lines snapped in a shower of white sparks and the pylon sagged at the waist. Its sturdy base did not budge but the top lurched, sagged and then gave way completely. The arms that had held the cables came crashing down to the ground so that the whole structure bent double. The long chain of identical steel skeletons stretching over the Pennines now had a broken link.

Watching the fireworks, Craig muttered, "My God!" With sore eyes, he squinted at his Land Rover. He was amazed to see it rocking from side to side. Still, it was the safest place to be.

The gale wrenched a satellite dish from the television

mast. It hit the ground and then bowled along like a drum on its side until it too went over the edge and out of sight. An aluminium panel came out of nowhere, rampaging across the fields, straight at Craig. Spotting it, he dived to the ground and the metallic sheet careered over his head. At the same time, the wind hurled a road sign like a spear into the side of his four-wheel drive.

Craig understood why some people thought of severe weather as a weapon. Even this storm – a mere tiddler on the world stage – had taken out the area's power supply and launched all sorts of makeshift weapons at him. Struggling back to his feet once again, he leaned into the gale and made for the protection of his Land Rover. He walked in slow motion. Every step was an effort, like wading waist-deep through water with a current that threatened to sweep him away. The storm knocked the breath out of him.

Pummelled by the wind, Craig looked through the driver's window and noticed that his laptop had just registered a top surge of 124 mph. It was the last thing he saw. Something came out from behind the Land Rover and, before he realised what was happening, took his legs away. He crumpled to the ground and, a few seconds later, he was tumbling helplessly over the edge and down the bank, followed by a large, plastic-wrapped bale of hay.

It wasn't just the weather that had put him in danger. It was also the success of his computer model.

CHAPTER 2

Twelve thousand metres above them, cirrocumulus clouds formed icy wisps of rippling hair in an immense blue sky. Drifting sedately across the horizon, five kilometres from the ground, a line of light altocumulus looked like blobs of high-flying cotton wool. Nothing threatened rain. The weather forecaster on the telly had got it right when she'd promised a sunny day with, at worst, a moderate breeze.

Brightly, Jake's mum announced, "Right, everybody out. The weather's beautiful."

At the age of eight, Jake Patmore was a funny little boy. He glanced upwards, then shook his head.

Carly sighed at her son. "What do you mean, no?"

He didn't respond.

"Come on, Jake," his mum said. "It's a shame to waste such a nice day. A walk in the hills will be great." She glanced at her parents and added, "Won't it?"

"Yes," they said in unison, obediently.

Grumpily, Jake turned his back, went to the understairs cupboard and extracted his cagoule.

Carly laughed. "You won't need that."

"Will."

"Won't," his mum retorted playfully.

"Will."

The whole pantomime audience – Grandma and Grandad – joined in. "Won't!"

Jake made a face. He was out-voted but he was also stubborn. He clung on to his cagoule and refused to let go, like a dog with a gloriously smelly bone. "You'll see," he muttered.

Carly had been expecting this day. Dreading it. Jake had always been obstinate and obsessed with the weather, but this was the first time he'd dared to insist that he knew best. His manner reminded her so much of his father. Pained at the thought of Craig and his dreadful accident two years ago, she took a deep breath. "All right," she said, yielding. "Out we go – with Jake's raincoat, just in case. Are you taking your camera as well, Jake?"

Jake frowned. "Not worth it."

"Oh, aren't you the grumpy one? Come on, you can put your cagoule in the boot."

He wouldn't even do that. He sat with the water-proof coat across his lap, grasping it possessively in his fist.

Later, despite the experts' forecast, the sky's smile turned into a scowl. Appearing from nowhere, flat and featureless altostratus whitewashed the sky. Then heavy nimbostratus rolled thickly over the Peaks,

13

blotting out the sun. The massive grey cloud was saturated with droplets of water. Below the main layer, ragged shreds of cloud reached down to the ground, blurred by rainfall.

Jake was the only one to return dry from their walk in the hills.

CHAPTER 3

It was Monday 1st May, two days after his fifteenth birthday. Jake stared down at five pages of untidy handwriting clasped in his quivering fingers. "What is this?"

The woman behind the desk answered dryly, "Exactly what it looks like. A letter from your father."

"But . . ." Jake shook his head in turmoil. He knew it was a letter from his dad. The solicitor had already told him. And he could see it for himself. On the fifth page at the bottom were two magical, fantastic, unbelievable words. *Love, Dad.* When he'd asked, "What is this?" he'd meant, "How can it be? How could I get such a letter? Where has it come from?" As far as he knew, heaven didn't have a postal service. In his hand, the pages trembled like leaves on a windy autumn day. He wasn't sure his fingers had the strength to hang on to them.

"You're fifteen, Jake, and my instructions were straightforward. If anything happened to Craig Patmore, subsequent to his writing this letter, I was to hand it to you – and you alone – as soon as possible on or after your fifteenth birthday."

"So, he wrote it before he died." Jake stopped, cursing his inability to say something sensible. Of course Dad wrote it before he died. "I mean, he wrote it ages ago."

"Yes. The letter's dated, I believe. 1997."

"Who knows about it?"

"You and me."

"No one else?"

"No," the solicitor replied.

"Not even Mum?"

"No one."

Jake fidgeted in his seat and swallowed. "Do I read it?"

The solicitor smiled in sympathy at Jake's bewilderment. "I imagine that would be your father's wish."

"I mean, here?"

"If you like. But it's your letter now. You can take it away and do with it as you wish. You can read it here or anywhere else. It's up to you."

"Have you read it?"

"No. It's a personal letter from a client to his son. If Mr Patmore had wanted me to share its contents, he'd have instructed me to read it and make a copy. I had no such instructions. There are no copies."

"I'll . . . um . . ." Jake folded the sheets and pushed them back into the envelope. He thrust the letter deep into a pocket and mumbled, "Thanks." He got up to leave.

"Are you all right, Jake?"

He shrugged.

"It must be a shock, after all these years."

"Yes."

The letter was a cold snowflake, drifting down from a troubled sky. Jake wasn't sure if he should marvel at its existence and beauty, or fear the storm that it might herald. He knew only that he wanted to be left alone to read it.

Not quite alone. When Jake plonked himself down on the edge of his bed, TC came to him in that jerky way of walking, looked at him with sad eyes and then rolled over. But Jake, distracted, did not reach down to tickle TC's stomach. He extracted the handwritten pages from the old envelope. The letter was the ragged scrawl of someone used to writing only with keypads. That was his dad, all right. Information technology had been his job, after all. Jake was eager to read his dad's message but he also dreaded the words that should have been cremated long ago. Putting off reading them for as long as possible, he showed the heirloom to TC. "Look. A letter from Dad. A secret letter."

The dog stared at the pieces of paper.

Jake looked at the date – top right – and added, "It's nine years old. Written when I was six. That was just before his accident." Jake stared up at the ceiling for a few seconds, then he added, "This is a big thing for

17

me, you know." Gathering his strength, he tried to force himself to read it. But his hands fell into his lap, along with the pages. "Who writes a letter in case they die?" he muttered. "Someone really worried or completely bonkers." Jake had a picture of his dad in his head. It was a good picture. A great picture. Superhuman Dad. He didn't want anything to spoil it. "I don't want to find out he was a nervous wreck or nuts," he said aloud to TC.

The dog inclined his head to one side, listening.

Jake couldn't put it off any longer. He breathed in deeply and lifted the papers with shaking hands.

Dear Jake

I am your baby-sitter tonight. Your mum has gone out. You're lying there asleep, looking innocent and peaceful. Not like me. I owe you some answers. Besides, adults are supposed to know everything, aren't they? That's the deal. You grow up and learn the ways of the world from us. But I feel inadequate because I don't know a lot and I'm not sure I'm going to be around anyway. I think I'm going to fail you.

If you're reading this, you'll be fifteen and I won't be around. You should have discovered by now that you have a way with the weather. It's a skill that runs in my family. You are very special – the latest in a long line of weather prophets.

When you think about it, the weather is the most

powerful force on the planet. It exists everywhere for all time and none of us can escape it. All life on Earth lives at its mercy – from a daisy to a polar bear to a human being. Populations thrive or die at the whim of its droughts, floods, storms, heat or cold.

As I write this, I wonder what form your gift will take. I dearly wish I could be around to see for myself and offer you my advice – for what it's worth – on how best to use it. We had an ancestor who was revered by early farmers and travellers for predicting the weather accurately. Your grandad is brilliant at forecasting but he says his knack is too dangerous to use so he keeps very quiet about it. Even so, he is weather-wise.

My ability, as your mum will have told you, involves computers. I developed Castleton Computing's model of the weather system. Of course, the weather is a complicated and chaotic system. It cannot be forecast exactly but my computer model is pretty good. I have even begun to program it to predict the outcome of a deliberate modification of the weather. Maybe it's <u>too</u> good. Recently, the model has locked me out of some parts of its programming. Some high-up in Castleton will be behind that. I'm bothered by the company's motives. Really, I'm more than bothered. Your mum tells me I'm neurotic but, since you're reading this, it probably means I wasn't. You will know I had good reason to be concerned.

All sorts of people have been to Castleton to see and

test the model. I'm sure some of them, like the Americans who turned up the other day, are in the military. I developed this computer model as the first step to preventing the misery, damage and death that extreme weather can bring. I didn't do it so storms could be aimed at people on purpose. If you could develop the ability to steer a hurricane away from a highly-populated area, any decent person would think of it as a blessing because it would prevent death and damage. To the military, though, it looks like a way of delivering a multi-megaton weapon to a specific target. If one country wanted to invade another, it would suit them to do it just after massive storms had weakened the opposition's troops.

Do you need convincing? Twenty-two years ago, Typhoon Nina dumped 1.6 metres of rain near Shanghai and killed 100,000–200,000 Chinese. Kick-starting a storm like that would be as deadly and effective as a nuclear bomb. Would America or Britain have the will to develop it? I think so. Enlisting the weather in time of war is hardly new. In ancient times, wizards used to burn magic dust to stop rain and make their enemies die of thirst. Medicine men danced around totem poles to conjure up lightning bolts against rival tribes. Even Moses asked God to strike at his foes from the heavens. In the 1960s and 70s, the US Department of Defense tried to manipulate lightning strikes in Project Skyfire and control the paths of hurricanes in Project Stormfury. Then *there was the infamous Operation Popeye in Vietnam between 1967 and 1972. Check it out.*

Here's the problem. If the weather becomes a weapon, a weather prophet becomes a prized soldier. I will not do that.

But I have not convinced your mum that Castleton might want to sell the atmosphere as a piece of military hardware. Maybe I'm wrong, but the company will not listen to me or answer my questions. Perhaps I <u>am</u> neurotic, but I'm disturbed by Castleton's reaction to me. It's suspicious, and borders on being threatening.

This is where I have to admit I don't have all the answers. I don't know the right way to deal with the situation. But I'm not going to let Castleton turn the sky into some sort of military laboratory. I'm going to put an end to their misuse of my computer model. Sabotaging my own work is the only way for me to feel better about myself and to stop my gift becoming a curse. But I don't know if I'm doing the right thing.

I don't know what you will do with your ability to read the signs of the weather. I have only one bit of advice. Follow your instinct. If the whole world is telling you what to do with your gift and it doesn't feel right to you, don't do it. Don't go beyond your comfort zone. Be prepared to turn your back on them all if you are uneasy with what people want from you.

I'm not sorry that I have passed on a demanding gift to you through my genes – it's a marvellous thing – but

I am sorry if I leave you to cope with it by yourself. Still, you'll probably make a better job of it than I have. Looking at you lying here now, I'm sure you will. You're capable of anything.

Love, Dad.

Jake sniffed and blinked away his tears. Reading the letter was almost like hearing his dad's voice in the room. But Jake's feeling of being close to his father did not last long. It was an illusion; he was close only to the ghost of his father. This letter was solid evidence – cruel evidence – that he was separated from his dad for ever by an unbridgeable rift. Still, the message itself was a shadowy bond between them that no one else knew about. And that made it special because it was his and his alone.

Eager now, he read the letter again as TC looked on.

Yes, Jake *had* always had a fixation with the weather. For him, the sky was a giant weather station. Finely tuned to it, he could look at the clouds, feel the wind, temperature and humidity, and he could predict what was coming. He could look at a weather map on the telly and know what the highs and lows, the troughs and ridges would bring. He had the same information as the forecasters but somehow he read much more from it. His interpretation of the information was always uncannily accurate. He'd never thought about it much – or tried to explain it. To Jake, it was simply

22

intuition. When mathematicians added two fives, they didn't actually work it out. They just looked at the sum and knew the answer: ten. In his first eight years of life, Jake had observed which cloud formations led to what sort of weather. He'd learned the basic equations and now, like a mathematician, he just knew the answers.

Four years ago, when the TV weatherman had been showing the path of Hurricane Isadora, threatening the Yucatan region of Mexico, Jake had jumped off his chair and run up to the screen. His bent finger against the glowing chart showed how he expected the hurricane to swerve into the Gulf of Mexico. The next day it did – swinging unexpectedly, missing Yucatan and instead slamming into Tampico in the centre of the Gulf of Mexico, just as Jake had predicted.

Last week, his mum had been going to get up in the middle of the night to watch a total eclipse of the moon. Jake had told her not to bother because the event would be totally shrouded in cloud. He was right. The next day, the newspapers carried no photographs of the celestial coincidence, only eerie silhouettes of disillusioned and fogbound stargazers.

That sort of thing happened to him all the time.

And today, belatedly, his dad had given him a special label that proved it. He was a weather prophet.

CHAPTER 4

So, was his dad crazy, a nervous wreck, or a hero? Jake couldn't tell from the letter but he *did* know that his father had taken a stand against Castleton Computing on a matter of principle. That fitted Jake's mental picture exactly. Jake felt proud of him. But Dad must have believed he was putting himself at risk or he wouldn't have written the letter in the first place. So, after lodging it with his solicitor, had he done something at Castleton to make himself a martyr? Would he really have risked that, with Jake depending on him? And would the company really have gone that far to stop him sabotaging his own weather model?

Maybe Jake was getting carried away. Maybe his dad had suffered an accident, just as his mum had claimed. She hardly said anything about it but she did tell him that his dad had taken a tragic tumble from the moors while researching awesome weather.

At least Jake understood why Dad hadn't typed his letter. Almost certainly, he wouldn't have wanted to leave a trace of his suspicions on a computer.

It crossed Jake's mind that his father might have

imagined the whole thing. After all, it sounded absurd to use the weather as a weapon. But almost at once Jake dismissed the notion that his dad was deluded. If Dad said it was happening, that was good enough for Jake.

Jake's father had not lived long enough to show his son that he was merely human, as fallible as any parent. In Jake's eyes he was still perfect. The letter hadn't destroyed his image.

One thought nagged at Jake. If his dad hadn't gone against Castleton, he might be alive today. Given the choice, Jake might have preferred a cowardly living father over a courageous dead one. He could be proud of a ghost but he couldn't go shooting photographs with one. For that, a father had to have flesh and blood. Jake could talk to a ghost in the way that he talked to TC but, for a response, a father had to be alive.

Jake sighed and looked down at TC. "I just wish I could remember him properly." There were photos around the house, of course, but his mum's photographs were her memories, not Jake's. And Mum – always bubbling, always in a good mood – never mentioned him, anyway. "Maybe Mum's forgotten him and moved on. But I haven't." Jake sighed and decided to keep the letter to himself.

Perhaps he'd inherited more from his dad than a way with the weather. With a wry smile, Jake wondered if he was barmy by birthright. Everyone said he was strange, a bit of a loner. Jake knew he wasn't like other boys. He guessed now it came with being a weather prophet. Maybe he couldn't have one without the other. Yet he didn't mind if he *was* a bit crackers. He didn't mind at all. It meant that he was closer to his dad.

Jake's bedroom was a shrine to the weather, ordinary and extraordinary. On the walls, there were lots of photographs, some out of magazines, many he'd taken himself over the years. Feathery hoarfrost on exposed tree roots, an on-rushing tornado like a demented rope, a starry snow crystal, the birth of cumulus on the horizon ahead of a warm front, a rainbow, a view of the globe from a weather satellite, a sinister shroud of radiation fog over the Peaks. Jake gazed at the most dramatic and horrifying of his pictures: a radar image of Hurricane Mitch just before the awesome swirl devastated Honduras and Nicaragua, erasing 11,000 lives. Yes. Some weapon. He shuddered.

It was then that Jake remembered something. It was his dad's reference to Typhoon Nina. He put the letter down on the bed, grabbed one of his old exercise books and flicked through the pages until he found some notes that he'd written years ago. He'd copied the facts from a textbook or a download off the Internet.

BLOW!
Hurricanes, Typhoons and Tropical Cyclones
Deep depressions formed over warm ocean water caus-ing wind speeds of over 74 mph/119 kph. They are called

hurricanes in the Atlantic, Caribbean Sea or northeast Pacific Ocean; typhoons in the northwest Pacific Ocean; and tropical cyclones in the southwest Pacific or Indian Ocean.

8th September 1900: Hurricane destroyed half of Galveston, Texas, and the storm surge took 8,000 lives, about a third of the city's population.

12-13th November 1970: 300,000 drowned in Bangladesh through tropical cyclone.

August 1975: Typhoon Nina dropped 1.6 metres/63 inches of rain in three days and two huge reservoirs burst, killing over 100,000 people in China.

Jake closed the notebook, shocked by the devastation he'd recorded. When he'd written those details, he must have been fascinated by numbers. Great big numbers of casualties. But numbers were just numbers. They were terrifying but impersonal. Somehow, the death of one person he'd heard of – or the death of one relative – meant much more than a whopping number. Still, Typhoon Nina had obviously made an impact on both father and son. The cruel storm was another link between them.

Jake took his dad's letter again, folded it and then hid it in the fifth book on the left hand side of his middle bookshelf, between pages 100 and 101.

Behind him, TC watched as if Jake were burying a bone for him to unearth later.

*

After sunset, the lower clouds were dark silhouettes against the glowing pink cirrus above them. Standing by the kitchen window for a while, Carly watched Jake in the back garden, trying to capture the colourful effect with his camera. Deciding to join him, she went outside. Staring into the night sky, Carly said reverentially, "It's gorgeous, isn't it?"

"Bad weather's coming."

The spectacular lines of jet-stream cirrus meant that the westerly wind at the top of the troposphere was blowing ferociously. A deep depression was on its way.

Carly gazed into her son's face, a young version of Craig's. "It's complex, the weather. It can't be predicted like . . . I don't know . . . which way an apple will fall off a tree: down every time. Forecasters can get tomorrow right sometimes, but not next month. It's unpredictable."

Jake took his eye off his camera and looked at his mum. "I know what's coming."

"Yes, but I haven't got the foggiest how. It's uncanny. You're one of the universe's great mysteries," she replied with a smile. On purpose, she had never encouraged him to broadcast his ability to predict the weather.

"Dad worked on the weather with a computer."

Carly hesitated, then nodded.

"What about *his* dad? Other Grandad."

"Haven't seen him in years. He's a bit of a recluse."

Jake said, "But is he weather-wise?"

Carly frowned for a moment. "Weather-wise? I haven't heard it put like that for ages. Why do you want to know?"

"I was just wondering. Is he?"

"I think so," Carly answered, shivering. "It's turning chilly out here now the sun's gone down."

"I ought to get myself tested."

Taken aback, Carly grimaced. "What? Why?"

"I bet they'd pay me lots to do the weather on the telly."

"I don't think there's a weather forecasting exam."

"I didn't mean that," Jake snapped.

"I know. But you don't really want meteorologists doing research on you."

"Don't I?"

Carly groaned inwardly. She knew from experience that arguing was no use. When Jake made a decision for himself, nothing would dissuade him. Sometimes she could get him to agree that what he was planning was daft, but he'd do it anyway. Sometimes he'd promise to drop an idea and, days later when she finally allowed herself to believe she'd won the argument, he'd resurrect it and crack on without telling her. It was as if Jake had to experience everything first-hand to discover what was a good idea and what wasn't. Carly's warnings to the baby Jake that fire hurt skin were not enough. He had to put his hand into the flame

29

to check if she was right. Now she knew that he'd hurdle or squirm around whatever barriers she placed in front of him. Fearing that he'd follow too closely in his father's footsteps, Carly could forbid his latest whim, but it would be pointless. "Well, you could write to the Met Office or the BBC, I guess," she said at last.

But Jake's expression told her that he'd seen straight through her. He knew she was suggesting something that was bound to fail.

"I've got to prove what I can do first." Quickly, he lifted up the camera, checked the display, and captured the sky before the colour faded as the sun dropped further below the horizon. "How do I do that?"

Carly was a computer programmer at Castleton, where she'd first met Craig. The company employed her to develop new software for controlling robots. She was certain that she didn't want Jake investigated by the company's meteorologist. Jake wouldn't want to work with Craig's replacement at Castleton, she was sure and, besides, she had good reason to keep a distance between Jake and Castleton Computing. But she did know an academic in the Department of Natural Sciences down the road at the university. Occasionally, Castleton had funded some of his research but he was independent of the company. Conceding, she said, "I guess I could make a phone call."

"Good."

*

Jake's dad had written his letter in 1997, before the Internet had taken off. Back then, in the Dark Ages, he probably wouldn't have guessed that a fifteen-year-old Jake would be able to log onto a Worldwide Web and search for information on Operation Popeye in 0.31 seconds.

Sitting in front of his mum's computer, Jake said to TC, "Hey. This is hot stuff. Dad was right. Listen: *'The US military mounted Operation Popeye in 1966 as a secret attempt to disrupt enemy supply lines in North Vietnam by inducing heavy rains and typhoons. The aim was to extend the monsoon season, thereby increasing the amount of mud on the Ho Chi Minh trail and inhibiting enemy movements. With the aid of satellite photographs, US aircraft flew into heavy cloud over the region and dispersed particles of silver iodide to seed rainfall. Twelve hundred rainmaking flights were conducted from 1967 to 1972. While the success of the operation remains controversial, some scientists believe Operation Popeye resulted in the unusually severe storms of 1971 and a significant reduction in the enemy's ability to bring supplies into South Vietnam.'*"

Jake took a breath, hardly able to believe what he was reading. He scrolled down the page. "*'When the United Nations found out about this new type of warfare that, with refinement, could threaten large tracts of the planet, they tried to stall its deployment. In 1978, the UN passed the Convention on the Prohibition of Military or Any Other Hostile Use of Environmental Modification*

Techniques (ENMOD). However, given the rate at which America has pulled out of conventions recently (e.g. treaties on biological weapons, landmines, nuclear testing, and global warming), this UN agreement may not survive. It is known that research into control of the weather has continued in the USA and UK. Such work is legitimate if it is carried out for peaceable purposes but not if it is done with hostile intent.'"

Jake swivelled round in the chair and looked at TC. "Phew! Makes you think, doesn't it? That was thirty-odd years ago. Makes you wonder what they're up to now."

CHAPTER 5

To an ordinary boy, the diagrams would have been meaningless circles and squiggles but Jake could read them like the contours of a map. The man from the university was laying out weather charts on the living-room floor. They recorded atmospheric conditions over England every six hours on two autumn days. He had blocked out the date and year. TC sat still in the corner, not leaping onto the tempting pieces of paper because he'd been told to stay where he was and he never disobeyed an order.

When Dr Robert Goodhart finished, he said to Jake, "The sequence starts there – top, left – and ends down here. Have you seen these particular charts before?"

Jake shook his head.

"OK. This is just a quick check – not a proper test – but it'll help me work out where you are. It's like finding out someone's level of reading before setting them a book. The question is, what happens the next day?"

It didn't take long to see it. The packed isobars and a huge frontal depression gave it away. Jake could see the circles tightening like a noose around the counties south of London by midnight. His hand wafted over the Channel and southern England. "Not just bad wind. Really bad – like a hurricane. Here."

Impressed, Dr Goodhart nodded. "Very good. Officially, it was a gale-force wind – but everyone called it a hurricane," he said. "And when the Met Office saw these charts, they got it wrong, talking more about heavy rain. The Great Storm of 1987."

Jake recalled writing notes about it.

HOMEGROWN

The Great Storm of 1987. 15-16 October. Changed the face of Sussex, Surrey and Kent by flattening fifteen million trees. Sevenoaks became 'Oneoak' because six of its famous trees blew over. The storm caused 19 deaths, brought road chaos by turning lorries over, demolished several properties, and knocked out London's power. Cost of damage: £1 billion.

Dr Goodhart smiled and said, "Your mum tells me you hardly ever get the weather wrong. She relies on you to know when to hang the washing out, tackle outside painting, or plan a barbeque."

Jake nodded.

"But mums are biased, I have to say. We need to do some proper research."

Jake could tell that the scientist was intrigued by him. He was also fascinated by TC because he kept glancing across the room at the obedient dog. Jake explained. "He's Mum's. She programmes robots at work. This one's a pet. Name of Tin Can, but we call him TC."

"Amazing. He's got the charm of a puppy – in a metallic sort of way."

"Mum says people treat small robots like they're animals so he's made to look like one. He's a guard dog as well. If someone attacked me . . ." Jake shook his head and pulled a face.

Jake recalled the first time he'd stroked TC. The robot had rolled over just like a real dog, expecting its tin tummy to be tickled. Thinking it was a mere toy, the young Jake giggled and said in a silly voice, "Does Tin Can want a nice drink of oil? How about a battery to eat?"

His mum smiled but remained serious for a change. "He's a security device, a guard dog, if you like. And more."

"He?"

"It, really. But," she added, "I think of him as male. I guess I do with all dogs until someone tells me theirs is a girl . . . I mean, female."

"Is he house-trained?"

"Very funny."

Jake looked from mechanical hound to mum. "If he's a guard dog, what does he do?"

"Lots. If you're worried about someone outside, just say, 'Lock doors.' He can lock and unlock them at a distance, like you do with car keys."

"Does he attack?"

She answered, "He can, yes. In the usual doggy way or with a few tricks."

"Does he go nuclear?"

"Let's not get too silly, Jake. He can let out clouds of smoke so an intruder can't see a thing in the house."

"Does he bark?"

Carly had nodded. "He's programmed with all sorts of doggy behaviour. He's got a speaker and different types of bark on a memory chip."

"What makes him attack?"

"I can order him to, verbally. And he can recognise threatening signs. Like someone coming towards either of us with a gun or a knife."

Jake had thought about this for a few seconds. "What happens when you ask me to give you the bread-knife and I walk towards you with it? Does he take my hand off?"

"No. He'll ignore it because it's within the family."

Jake went silent again for a while, and then he said, "So I can murder you and get away with it."

"Let's not let any disagreements get that far," his mum said, laughing.

"What if I'm wearing a hoodie when I give you the knife? Will he recognise me then?"

"Don't worry. He doesn't need a face. Right now, he's learning your size, how you walk, your voice. He's got lots of recognition capabilities."

Jake soon took to TC. He could see why people would treat a robot as a live pet. It was because TC seemed to have moods and intentions like a real animal. But he didn't. He had only clever programming and artificial intelligence where a flesh-and-blood dog had free will.

His mum had explained. "If he looks happy or sad or hurt, he's just mimicking what he sees in us. He's got rules like: if Jake comes towards me looking happy, act happy; if Jake comes towards me looking sad, act sad. Hundreds of rules. Shout at him, tell him off, and he'll react like you do when I tell you off. He's just programmed to pick up human behaviour and add it to his doggy repertoire. That way, we can relate to him better. It doesn't mean he's got feelings. He isn't capable of feeling anything."

So Jake acquired a best friend who was always faithful and obedient, who never argued, who listened to him whenever he wanted to talk, and who never felt let down because he didn't have feelings. It was like having an imaginary friend – or an imaginary father.

Robert Goodhart was explaining the statistics of the coming tests to Jake. "If I say it's going to rain tomorrow, it's just a guess. I might get it right or I might get it wrong. If I do it a hundred times, I'd get about fifty right and fifty wrong. Like tossing a coin, it's a fifty-fifty chance. Yes? So, if I ask you to predict the weather once and you get it right, it might be down to luck. Scientifically, it doesn't mean anything. If I ask you a hundred times and you score eighty hits or more, well, that'd be extraordinary. So, every day, I'll email the latest weather chart to you and you email me back your forecast. And, in case you're wondering, I'm not daft. I'll be checking what you say against the official outlook in case you're cribbing."

"Huh."

"Huh?"

"More likely, *they'll* want to crib from *me*."

Robert grinned, amused by the boy's confidence. "We'll see."

Jake had inherited a miniature weather station from his dad. Looking like a beehive in the back garden, the bright white box with slatted sides contained a maximum-minimum thermometer and a hygrometer for measuring humidity. A rain gauge was attached to the fencepost nearby and, a few metres above it, there was a weather vane and anemometer for checking wind direction and strength.

Jake had a morning and evening ritual. He took readings from the weather box. He had a good look at the clouds in the sky, estimating the amount of cover, their height, type and movement. He noted the wind conditions. He logged any signs of moisture: rain, snow, drizzle, hail, mist, dew, frost. And indoors, he recorded atmospheric pressure from the large barometer in the hall.

Now, he added one more activity to his routine. Every morning, he consulted Robert Goodhart's emailed weather map. It was the final piece of an ever-changing jigsaw that he solved somehow every day. While other forecasters constructed only a fuzzy view of the future, Jake's vision was crystal clear.

After two weeks, Dr Robert Goodhart tried but failed to contain the excitement in his voice. Even on the phone, he was as easy to read as one of his emailed weather charts. "Yes, it's going very well. Excellent, in fact. You haven't got one wrong yet. I want to bring someone else to see you, Jake. Is that all right?"

"Yes." Jake didn't mind who it was. He liked being the centre of attention and he relished another opportunity to impress. Besides, he'd begun to enjoy making waves. His days of hanging out, waiting for something to happen, were over. He'd decided he was going to take on the big, frightening and exciting world. It was time to stop clinging to Mum. He hadn't cut that umbilical cord until now because he'd had no idea what he was going to attach it to instead. But his dad had provided the answer. With his gift for weather forecasting, he could have an impact. He could find his place in the world and accomplish something.

"Thursday afternoon? After school?" asked Dr Goodhart.

"OK, but . . ."

"What's the problem?"

Jake said, "There'll be thunder and lightning. And hail. Serious stuff."

"That's not what the Met Office is forecasting."

"They're wrong."

Robert laughed. "You know, I'm beginning to believe you. I'll bring an umbrella."

Jake put the phone down, muttering to himself, "An umbrella won't do any good."

CHAPTER 6

At school, Jake Patmore was invisible. He wasn't one of the bad boys and he wasn't a shining angel. He wasn't a highflier and he wasn't special needs. He was neither particularly popular with his peers, nor was he disliked. He wasn't the first or the last player to be picked for a sports team. No extremes for Jake, neither scorching equatorial sunshine nor polar ice. No piercings, no tattoos. He was just ordinary, run of the mill. Except at Geography.

All of the kids liked the Geography teacher. "Cosmic" Cosgrove was young, always grumbling at the dull curriculum that he was forced to teach, a fanatical supporter of Newcastle United and had once been caught smoking on the playing field with the post-sixteens. For Jake, Cosmic was perhaps the nearest thing he had to a father figure.

The nearest thing Jake had to a best mate was Aidan Webb. Back in Year 7 – at the time of Hurricane Isadora – Jake found himself sitting next to Aidan when the English teacher was giving him an earful for the quality of his homework. Aidan had shrugged and said, "Someone's got to be bottom. The school's lucky to have me as a willing volunteer." They'd been friends ever since.

Aidan had a full set of parents. They were separated, but not as separated as Jake's mum and dad. Aidan lived with his mother – that is, he occupied the same house but avoided being in the same room – and most weekends his dad took him to the Sheffield United match. Aidan wasn't bothered about football but his dad was mad keen. He claimed it was a manly thing they could share. Actually, Aidan's thing was music. Jake had seen it for himself in the school's Music Department. Given the right software and samples, the boy could really rock. At home, Aidan took himself to his bedroom, turned up his iPod, and stayed there.

Aidan was deeply embarrassed by his mum. She was a Parent Governor at the school, and a journalist. "Not even the *Sun* or the *Mail* or anything. Just some rubbish local rag. She's in the remedial class of reporters," Aidan moaned. When she came into school for a meeting, he would stay in the cloakroom. When she gave a careers talk to his class, he did his best to hide under the table.

Mrs Webb didn't seem so bad to Jake. She looked cool for an oldie.

Smelling Cosmic's stale-cigarette breath behind them now, Jake and Aidan both turned.

"How there. Nerds Anonymous meeting, is it?" Mr Cosgrove knew that Jake and Aidan were sometimes called the Nerds but neither their mates nor the Geordie teacher meant it nastily. It was almost affectionate. "Run along to your next lesson."

"But it's Maths, sir."

"Mmm, yummy," Cosmic replied.

"Boring," Aidan muttered. "And useless."

Cosmic shook his head. "Nonsense. We all need maths."

"I've got a gift," Jake said. "You know. Like a great footballer. Great footballers don't do algebra. All they know is football, goals and money. I'm weather-wise. There'll always be a forecasting job for me."

"And I'm going to be a DJ," Aidan put in.

"Aren't we getting ahead of ourselves? I hope you're both right, but what are you going to fall back on if your plans don't work out?"

"I'll never use Maths anyway," said Aidan grumpily. "Calculators and computers were specially invented for me."

Cosmic clutched their shoulders with his yellowed fingers and propelled both of the boys towards the door. "You never know. So get cracking."

As a parting shot, Jake said, "Don't leave your car outside Thursday afternoon."

STRIKE FORCE
Every day, 45,000 thunderstorms form over the planet.
HAIL. The British record of hailstone size is 9.5 cm

diameter (626 g). One hailstone in a thunderstorm that killed 92 people in Gopalganj, Bangladesh, in April 1986 weighed 1.02 kg. In Northern India in 1888, hailstones the size of cricket balls killed 246 people and 1,600 sheep and goats.

14 April 1999. The eastern suburbs of Sydney, Australia, experienced a monster thunderstorm for over 5 hours. The area was pelted with hailstones the size of apples. About 40,000 vehicles and 20,000 homes were damaged.

LIGHTNING. The intense heat of lightning is estimated to be 30,000°C. Most strikes are about 9 km in length but a bolt of 150 km was measured in the USA in 1956. Worldwide, there are about 100 lightning flashes every second. In Britain, there are roughly 300,000 ground strikes in an average year; about 45 people will be struck and 3 will be killed. Fatalities were far higher in previous centuries when more people worked outside, especially in farming.

As Thursday unfolded, the giant among clouds gathered. Cumulonimbus was the trademark for bad weather. It formed a dense towering column stretching from its dark base near the ground to a white top shaped like an anvil, fifteen kilometres up. Ragged clouds underneath the base shifted in different directions by gusts of wayward wind. Within the cloud, tiny particles of ice were carried upwards on the rising current of air, growing as they gathered droplets of water. Many of the frozen particles descended on the down-draught before climbing again in the water-rich updraught, engorging themselves with layers of ice. In minutes, they'd risen and fallen through the cloud several times as if they were stuck in an elevator. Sooner or later, they were flung out of the updraught or they became heavy enough to fall through it. On the ground, they arrived as hailstones, from the size of peas to golf balls, at 60 mph.

Even before reaching the Patmores' house, Jake's visitors must have been impressed. Jake had promised them a lively storm and they were arriving in the thick of it.

On the hill behind Jake's home, lightning struck the tallest tree. Hail brought down two telephone cables, and dented a few roofs and vehicles. One large hailstone cracked Dr Goodhart's windscreen. The storm also ruined his flimsy umbrella as soon as he got out of his car.

In the hall, the meteorologist shook himself like a drenched animal. "Phew!"

"I did say," Jake reminded him.

Robert smiled. "You did indeed. This," he said, turning to his companion who was wearing a pinstripe suit and a monstrous tie, "is Timo Scarpa."

"Yes?" Jake said, expecting more.

Timo stepped towards him and held out a hand.

"Sorry I'm a bit damp. I'm from Henson Insurance. We fund some of Dr Goodhart's work and he told us about you. He thought we'd be interested." Out of the corner of his eye, he spotted TC but he didn't seem surprised so Robert must have forewarned him about the family's robotic pet.

Jake led them to the living room. "Insurance?"

"Yes. We're an American company but we have outposts all over the place. I've come up from London."

Jake's eyebrows rose. "Why?" This man had come a long way in filthy weather for a few minutes with Jake?

Sitting down, Timo replied, "Well, I think *you're* more interesting to talk about than me, but I will say this. Insurance companies are more concerned about extreme weather than ever before. We've got to assess the risks of storm damage, flooding and that sort of thing." Glancing towards the window, he continued, "Even a storm like this will dent a few cars and cause urban disruption. Do you know what I mean? We'll have to pay out."

"Oh?"

"It's probably more than you think. The 1987 storm cost Henson millions. And it's much worse in America. Hail did six hundred million dollars' worth of damage in Denver, back in 1990. Hurricane Andrew cost us twelve billion dollars, around fifty deaths, a quarter of a million homes destroyed. Don't even get me started on floods and forest fires. My pacemaker couldn't cope. Let's just say they're not good for the insurance business. And it'll get worse if global warming picks up even more."

Jake was puzzled. "Why have you come to see me? I can't stop a hurricane."

Timo said, "You might be able to tell us when and where it'll strike – with enough time to minimise damage and get people out of harm's way."

Robert added, "When Hurricane Andrew got close to America, weather forecasters evacuated a million people from their homes. You don't do that lightly – and if you get it wrong . . ." He shook his head. "It's a big responsibility, Jake."

Suddenly, Jake realised he was already close to that money-spinning job he'd mentioned to Cosmic Cosgrove. "But I don't get it wrong," he said confidently. "I've passed all your tests, haven't I?"

"We're nowhere near through yet."

Timo leaned forward. "I've seen your emailed forecasts. Remarkable. How do you do it, Jake?"

"I look at the sky, feel the wind, smell the air, and I just know."

"No two skies are exactly the same so you can't simply be saying, 'I've seen this cloud formation before and I know what it brings.' You must be doing more than that."

"I take temperature, rainfall and pressure readings,

see what the wind's up to, and check out weather charts. I can do it that way as well, but I don't need to."

On the edge of his seat, Timo said, "You've been forecasting the weather for South Yorkshire and making a few wider predictions. Could you do, say, Tornado Alley – north Texas to Minnesota in America – if you had the charts?"

Jake shrugged. "Never tried. I don't see why not."

Timo took a CD from his suit pocket and asked, "Can we use your computer?"

The downstairs bedroom had become a study long ago. Jake took them into the cramped room, where pellets of ice still pounded the window. He was about to switch on his mum's computer when Robert stopped him.

"Is there going to be any more lightning, Jake? If there is, it's too dangerous to turn it on. You can be struck through the wires."

Jake shook his head. "The lightning's moved away. It's OK."

While the machine loaded, Timo explained, "On here, I've got weather maps, tables, photos and satellite images of four weather systems near Oklahoma. They were all taken about this time of year – May and June – in the afternoon. That's rush hour for tornadoes in the Midwest. What I want to know is, which developed into full-blown tornadoes? It could be all four or none of them. I don't know." He told Jake to double-click on the compact disk icon and open the file called *Tornado Test*.

As images of billowing cumulonimbus decorated the monitor, Jake said, "If you don't know, how are you going to tell if I get it right?"

Timo waved his mobile. "There's a man at head-quarters who knows. I'm kept in the dark so you can't pick up any clues from my manner."

"I haven't done this before," Jake muttered as he examined the first weather map. "I've never even seen a tornado for real."

Speaking above the din of the storm, Robert said, "Believe it or not, Britain holds the world record for the most tornadoes per land area, but most are too weak and brief to be noticed. Not all twisters are violent."

The two men and TC stood behind Jake as he went through the tables of temperature, wind direction, humidity and pressure, the photos and charts.

With a sinking feeling, Jake slowly realised that he didn't know what he was looking for. His intuition told him that the first case was subtly different from the other three but he didn't know how to decipher his feeling. He turned towards his eager audience with a grimace. Outside, distant thunder growled.

Timo smiled at him. "Don't worry. Even experts can't predict them with any degree of certainty." Watched keenly by Tin Can, Timo leaned across Jake and clicked on a different icon. "If you like, we'll leave you to browse this. It's got examples of storms that produced tornadoes and some that didn't. Maybe they'll help you get a feel for it. Take as long as you like. We're not in a hurry."

Robert agreed. "We're hoping you're not going to throw us out till it's stopped chucking it down."

CHAPTER 7

Leaving him, the two men withdrew to the living room. Tin Can stood in the hallway between the two rooms so that he could keep watch on everyone. Jake knew the men were treating him like his mum treated TC – as a machine to be trained. When TC first had to learn how to recognise Jake, no matter what he was wearing or doing, the robot observed Jake's behaviour over several days and used the data to construct his own set of rules. It was called artificial intelligence. Now that Jake had to learn to recognise which thunderstorms developed into tornadoes, he examined Timo's weather profiles in the hope that he could use them to construct his own set of rules. Not artificial intelligence, but a reliable instinct.

Jake saw many elements that made up a tornado. A weather junction where the warm wet wind coming from the Gulf of Mexico collided with the mass of cold dry air from Canada, a warm body of air lying below a colder one, westerly jet streams high overhead, and the shrinking of a swirling thunderstorm at its southwest edge into a tighter circle, like an ice skater spinning faster and faster by folding her outstretched arms against her body. Then he looked at the width of torna-does, their speed, lifetimes and paths. It was bewildering and messy but, in Jake's weather-wise brain, a complex pattern was beginning to form.

After an hour, Jake walked into the living room and announced, "Only the first storm – Case A – became a tornado."

At once, a tense Timo Scarpa held up his mobile phone and said, "I'll check." Hesitating, he asked, "You're sure the lightning's over? I don't want to fry myself."

Jake nodded.

Timo turned on his mobile and called someone. When he'd finished listening, he grinned. "Three out of four is brilliant."

Jake frowned. "Only three?"

"Storm A was terrifying. Classified F5. Wind speed of three hundred miles an hour. It destroyed everything in its path. If a house had concrete foundations, that was the only thing left. But Storm C produced a twister as well . . ."

Interrupting, Jake asked, "Are you sure?"

Timo nodded. "To be fair, it was an F1. That's weak. It didn't go very far and it didn't do any damage. It was a minnow."

Quick as a flash of lightning, Jake defended himself. "So why would an insurance company want me to pre-dict a storm that does no damage?"

Timo laughed. "Point taken." Once more he sat upright on the edge of his seat. "And it's not the end of the good news. There's a network of Doppler radar detectors across the USA looking for signs of tornadoes. They're pretty good but they don't give much more than ten minutes' warning. You were looking at Storm A half an hour before it gave birth to a tornado." He paused to let the importance of advanced warning sink in. "But you still don't know how you worked it out, do you?"

Jake shook his head.

The insurer collapsed back into the easy chair. "Oh well. How you do it isn't as important as actually doing it. But it makes it harder for me to explain to the boss – and justify more tests."

"More tests?"

"If we sent you up-to-date weather charts for Tornado Alley, what would you need to let us know when you think a tornado's brewing?"

Jake pondered on it. He needed nothing at all, but he could think quickly when it really mattered. "I'd need my own computer with the best weather software and a broadband connection for downloading charts."

Timo smiled. "OK. I'll sort it out."

"Really?" Jake couldn't hide his surprise. It was so easy.

"Sure."

"And a TV dish and decoder for getting live weather views from satellites."

"All right."

"I'll tell you something else . . ." Jake began.

"What?"

TC tilted his head to one side. It was a behaviour he'd learned from humans when they were listening intently.

"My dad made a computer model of the weather. If I had a copy of that . . ."

The two men looked at each other significantly. It was Robert who replied. "We know about it. And we'd all like a copy but you're more likely to get an iceberg in the Caribbean. Castleton's got the copyright well and truly sewn up. Besides, to run it, you'd need a supercomputer worth a million."

"That's right," Timo agreed. "They've got at least a couple of private weather satellites up in orbit as well. We'd all like to get our hands on the information they beam back down to Castleton. But . . ." He shrugged. "It's not going to happen."

The two men stood up, clearly ready to go. In a particularly good mood, Timo asked, "Is it safe to go out now?"

Jake nodded. "No more storms here today."

Once he'd ushered the men out, he leaned against the front door and let out a long sigh. Then he shivered with anticipation. If he could develop more of a feeling for tornadoes, he could name his price to this Henson Insurance company. They coughed up millions, even billions, in insurance claims every time the weather wrecked lives, properties and possessions, so they'd save huge sums if he could alert them in time to evacuate people, their expensive belongings and their vehicles. His advice would be worth untold amounts of money.

Jake wasn't really greedy. He just wanted to buy the best weather gadgets and a top-of-the-range digital camera. If he had more money, he could also help out his mum. For the last nine years, they'd struggled to make do with her salary. Of course, money also proved his status as a weather prophet. To Jake, that meant just as much – maybe more – than having cash to spare.

Slowly wandering upstairs, Jake wondered how to tell his mum about the new tests when she got back from work. More importantly, he wondered what his dad would make of hanging out with an insurance company. In his bedroom, he clutched the fifth book on the left hand side of his middle bookshelf and flicked through it till he got to page 100. But there was nothing between the leaves. His dad's precious letter was gone.

CHAPTER 8

Increasingly agitated, Jake went through all of the nearby books as well. Nothing. Absolutely nothing. The letter really had vanished.

TC came into the bedroom after completing a slow and clumsy ascent of the stairs. Straight away, the robot mimicked Jake. He looked exasperated, like a famished dog whose food bowl was nowhere to be seen.

Distraught and baffled, Jake slumped on the bed. "Where the hell is it?" How could the letter have gone? And why? "It was addressed to me," he snapped. "No one else. Just me."

He looked around the room. The carpet was spotless for once. His mum must have opened his door to let loose the robotic vacuum cleaner that roved around the house like a cake tin on castors, sucking up muck. But, unless she'd been spying on him, she wouldn't be aware of the secret letter. It was even less likely that she'd know its hiding place. If she had somehow stumbled upon it, she would have said something. Actually, she would have said lots because she would have been hurt that Jake had kept it from her.

Who else had been in the house since the solicitor had given him Dad's letter? A few of his mum's friends, Aidan, Robert Goodhart, Timo Scarpa and that was it, as far as Jake knew.

Aidan was a friend, not a thief. The two meteorologists would have had an interest in the letter, and they could have slipped upstairs while he was looking through the tornado files. But it was likely that TC would have alerted him by barking if they had strayed from the living room. If they had begun to rummage around, Jake guessed that TC would have gone bonkers. One of his mum's visitors, Neisha Ray, also worked at Castleton Computing. Neisha might have been keen to see his dad's letter but Jake had no idea how she could have learned about it.

Jake stared down at TC, who was looking as distressed as Jake himself. "Is that all you can do?" Jake said crossly. "Get your batteries in a twist? It'd be better if you could give me a print-out of everyone who's been in here."

At once, TC hung his head, looking sheepish and hurt.

"Yeah. You're supposed to be a guard dog. Why didn't you guard it?"

There was a sudden loud thump downstairs. Jake jumped but, glancing at his watch, realised it was just his mum returning from work. She'd probably got her hands full of papers and slammed the door shut with her foot.

Her voice drifted upstairs. "Only me. I'm back."

As Tin Can headed for the stairs, Jake shouted, "Yeah." But he didn't feel like going down to meet her face to face. He wasn't in the mood now that his only lifeline to his father had been severed.

Over dinner, Jake decided to confront her. Yet he couldn't blunder in with an accusation of stealing. That way, he would have to let on about the ghostly message. He needed to steer the conversation so that she had an opportunity to own up if she'd lifted Dad's letter from his bedroom. But it wasn't easy. He didn't really do subtlety.

He wanted to scream, "Did you nick my letter?" Instead, restraining himself, he said, "I'm going to see Grandad Patmore."

Startled, his mum replied, "You're what?"

"Going to see Grandad Patmore."

"I don't think . . . Why?"

"I want to have a chat with him."

Carly put down her knife and fork. She finished off her first glass of wine and poured another to the brim. "Why?"

"He's weather-wise. Like me. You said so."

"I . . . er . . . OK. I guess you've got every right to see

him. He is your dad's dad after all. And I can't deny him the right to see you if he wants to. But . . ." She sighed, briefly lost for words. Trying to sound light-hearted, she continued, "Your grandad's so dotty, he almost put me off marrying your dad – in case he turned out the same. It didn't help that your grandma . . . Well, never mind. Anyway, your dad was different – very different – almost sane in comparison. He'd got some funny ideas about power over the weather but he wasn't in the same league as your grandad."

Jake didn't reply, hoping silence would force more information from her.

"He hasn't got a phone so you can't call or drop him an email."

Jake shrugged. "I'll just go – this weekend."

"I don't think it's a good idea, Jake – but you're not going to take any notice of what I think, are you?"

"No."

"Thought not." She smiled. "I won't come with you but you can get a bus to Barnsley. Check it out on the Internet. I'll pay."

Her refusal to accompany him suited Jake. He could have a good talk with his grandad, unhindered by his mum.

"Write him a letter tonight to tell him you're coming – and when."

"A letter?"

"Yes. You remember letters, don't you? They were what we did before mobiles and email."

There wasn't a trace of guilt on her face as she said it, convincing Jake that his mum wasn't behind the disappearance of his dad's note. Abruptly, Jake changed the subject. "Your friend, Neisha, who works with you at Castleton."

Carly frowned at the sudden shift. "Yes. What about her?"

"Is she a programmer as well?"

"Not really. She's in defence."

"Defence? What does that mean?"

"It means resisting attack," she replied, trying to lighten the exchange with good-humoured sarcasm. "What do they teach you in school these days?"

Jake sighed. He wasn't in the mood for joking. "I know what it means. What does she do?"

"Why the interest?"

Jake shrugged. "Nothing in particular. Just wondered."

"Castleton's not all about mechanical guard dogs and automatic domestic appliances. That's not where the money is. Some of the robots are designed to help out with defence. Robot soldiers to reduce troop casualties, autopilots for unmanned planes, all sorts."

Jake turned up his nose. He didn't approve. But at least it didn't seem to have anything to do with the weather – or the missing letter. Even if the military saw a storm as a brutal weapon to unleash against an enemy, no one could call it defence. It was attack. Anyway, he couldn't ask his mum if Neisha Ray had gone upstairs last time she'd visited. That would trigger a very awkward question in return.

Jake changed gear again and told his mum about Robert Goodhart's latest visit, Henson Insurance, tornadoes, and the free gifts. "And I've thought of something else to ask for."

Carly looked bewildered by the pace of developments. "What?"

"A tour of Tornado Alley would be nice. I bet I could get it if I asked."

"Hold on. What for?"

"To get a real feel for the weather. To chase some tornadoes."

"Jake," his mum said earnestly, "I think you've got to slow down and take stock. You certainly need to wait for me to catch up. You're talking like someone who's done with school, maybe even with university. You sound like you're muscling into a job. This is a big thing and you're too young."

"I'm not talking about leaving school. Summer holiday's coming up. You're always going on at me to find a job and earn some cash. A couple of emails will do it. I'll ask this insurance bloke for a summer forecasting job and an American holiday rolled into one. I bet he'll go for it."

Carly was shaking her head and smiling. "I can see you're keen and it's true a summer holiday job would be good for you. As long as that's all it is. If this man gives you the thumbs-up, I'll need to speak to him."

"He's in London."

"I think the telephone system stretches that far."

CHAPTER 9

The morning sunshine penetrated the overnight fog and heated the ground. Warmed, the air rose and lifted the mist, transforming it into stratus cloud. As Jake walked down the road on the outskirts of Barnsley, keeping an eye on the house numbers, he realised that his image of his grandad was falling apart. In his mind, Jake saw Grandad living the isolated life of a monk in the middle of nowhere. The old man's home would be a thatched cottage with ivy crawling all over it. No gas or electricity. Inside, there'd be oak beams, rickety furniture, and the smell of strange concoctions and candles. A fireplace and a huge antique clock with a loud tick and a deep chime like a death knell would dominate the living room.

It was nothing like. It was an unremarkable terrace in an unremarkable street, overlooking a park and farm that had once been a coal mine.

While the house was ordinary, Grandad Patmore wasn't. He wore a cap over his bald head and white wispy hair straggled around his large ears and neck. He didn't have a beard but he wasn't clean-shaven either. His leathery cheeks and chin were decorated with white stubble. Under bushy eyebrows, his eyes gave nothing away. He could have been delighted to see his grandson or he might have resented the intrusion. It was impossible to tell. A stocky man, the same height as Jake, he was wearing clothes that were at their best at least ten years ago. In his hand, he carried an air pistol.

"So, you're Jake," he said in a matter-of-fact voice, a deep Yorkshire accent.

Jake nodded.

"You're quite a lad now. Nothing like your dad."

"No." Jake had only his mum's photographs to judge, but he agreed.

"They used to say you look like him, but you don't."

Like Jake himself, Grandad focused on the differences and not the considerable similarities that everyone else saw.

The old man led Jake through the passage at the side of the house, into the lush back garden. Almost at once, he took aim with his pistol.

Open-mouthed, Jake cried, "Er . . . What are you doing?"

Grandad pointed. "Look. In the aspen tree. Vermin!"

"What?"

The bird took off before Grandad could fire the pellet. "Damn!" he muttered.

"It was just a pigeon," Jake said.

"Just?" Grandad shook his head in apparent exasperation. "I don't suppose that mother of yours has taught you how to shoot pigeons. Vermin."

"Er . . . No, she hasn't."

Grandad Patmore looked as if he were about to deliver a tirade against either pigeons or spineless modern ways, but he didn't. He frowned instead. "Let's go in. I'll open a window in case it comes back. I can get it from inside."

"Can you do that? Is it allowed?"

Grandad shrugged. "No one bothers if you shoot a rat. Pigeons are flying rats. Rodents with wings. Vermin. I'll shoot 'em if I want. It's my home, my choice, my right."

The house wasn't bristling with gadgets like Jake's place. It had only a decrepit radio and television.

"You said in your letter you wanted to talk about the weather and your dad. Your dad – God bless him – went right off the rails, lad. He got all technical. Computers! What do computers know? Nothing. They don't know about clouds, fog, rain and snow. They just add numbers. And numbers add up to nowt. What you want is an old-fashioned barometer, a thermometer, a bit of seaweed, a weather vane on the roof, and a garden. And the most important thing of all," leaning close as if whispering secrets, he pointed upwards, "clouds. You can read clouds like a book if you know their language. *When high clouds and low in different paths go, be sure that they show it'll soon rain and blow*. Do you need a computer?" He shook his head.

Grandad pointed out of the window where, every day, elements of the weather passed by in endless variety. "Outside. That's the only laboratory you need. Plants, animals and the sky. The sky's like the face of a friend. When you get to know him, you can analyse every line, every colour and texture, and know what he's going to do. Your dad lost touch with real weather. He wouldn't have known a gale if it had him pinned to a wall. And your mam's just as bad. Machines! That's why she hasn't kept in touch. She knows I'm no friend of her ways. I hope you've got more sense in you, lad." With barely a pause, he said, "You'll be wanting a mug of tea." And off he went to the kitchen.

Hardly daring to refuse the drink, Jake followed him.

"I'll tell you, lad," Grandad continued. "Folk aren't as sensitive to the weather as they used to be. They know *Red sky at night, shepherds' delight; red sky at morning, shepherds' warning*, and that's about their lot. It's because we've got roofs over us heads most of the time these days. Once, everyone worked the land or the sea. Them days, livelihoods rested on tomorrow's weather. Some of us haven't forgotten how to read the signs, though. I bet you can."

Jake nodded. "I'm having tests . . ."

"Tests!" Grandad exclaimed. "What use are tests? You know what you can do."

66

"Yes, but . . ." Jake sighed. "If you were tested and someone found out you were brilliant at singing, you'd go on stage, wouldn't you?"

"Would you? There's no law says you have to. If you had a knack for shooting, would you murder everyone?"

"No."

"There you are. If it's dangerous, you leave well alone," Grandad said.

"But it's just weather forecasting. There's no harm in it."

"Isn't there?"

Jake kept quiet while his grandad poured the boiling water.

In a hushed voice, the old man said, "They killed your dad, you know."

"What?"

"Believe me, they did."

"They? Who?"

"That company of his."

"Castleton."

Grandad nodded. "He was a daft bugger, mind. Going out in a storm like that. It's what I said. He'd know exactly what the wind speed was, but wouldn't have a clue what it *felt* like. Numbers, yes. Knowledge, no. And sense, no. But I'll tell you this. It wasn't the storm that pushed him over the edge. Pah!"

Wide-eyed, Jake asked, "Do you know this for sure?"

"Guaranteed."

"How?"

"It's nature." Grandad nodded towards the window. "See my silver maple? It always shows the lining of its leaves when a storm's coming, and the aspen's leaves tremble like they're scared. Pine cones close and flies turn sluggish before a storm. My feet feel cold ahead of snow, and my ears ring before a change in the weather. As for rain, I get a feeling of dread when it's on its way. *If the moon rises haloed round, soon you'll tread on deluged ground.* Dandelions and scarlet pimpernel know as well." He clenched his open palm into a fist slowly, saying, "They close their flowers before a downpour. Believe me, I know what's around the corner. I knew your dad's time had come." Taking Jake by surprise, his grandad took hold of Jake's shoulders and said, "Look at me."

Jake couldn't. He turned his face away.

His grandad shook him gently until Jake made eye contact. "Ah, I see."

"What?"

The old man let him go. "I see pride in you, lad. That's what the tests are all about. You're showing off. How old are you now?"

"Fifteen."

Grandad nodded knowingly. "That explains it." Without letting Jake get a word in, he said, "So, there's no harm in weather forecasting, eh, lad? Maybe not if it's to work out when to sow seeds, take off in a plane or set sail, but what happened to Follett Patmore? Look him up. He's one of your ancestors. And then there's your dad." Strangely, Grandad shook his head and smiled. "He couldn't abide me telling him, but there's hundreds of old sayings with more sense than them computers. *If there's ice in November that will bear a duck, there'll be nothing after but sludge and muck*." He laughed. "That's my favourite. *Swallows high, staying dry; swallows low, wet will blow*. Everything I know, your dad reckoned he had a scientific explanation for. He said, 'When it's fine, birds catch insects way up high. When a change is coming, the insects fly lower down so the swallows follow suit.' Science! But what makes the insects come down, eh?"

Jake thought that his grandad's wry smile hid something much more raw. He was probably making a show of his scorn for his son's ways so he did not have to reveal his softer side. Jake thought that Grandad was still angry about his son's death, still grieving in his own way. Taking the mug of tea, Jake said, "Thank you." As they walked back into the living room, he added, "You know, I don't remember anything about Grandma."

"No."

That was it. Nothing else. An impenetrable wall of fog came between them.

"Don't you have photos?"

"It was a long time ago."

Jake sat down, sipped the tea and changed the subject. "Dad said I was capable of anything."

"Oh?" Suddenly, Grandad was back with him. "Who told you that?"

"Dad. I got a letter from him. He got his solicitor to give it to me when I turned fifteen."

Grandad paused, then nodded. "Yes, that sounds like Craig all right. He must have written it when you were little. That means he knew folk were after him." He leaned towards Jake and added, "It's your letter. You keep it to yourself. But I'd like to see it. Just for . . . you know . . . just to hear him again – through the words he's written."

"I can't. Someone's taken it."

Grandad's face became tense. "What? That's . . . That'll be that Castleton. You take care, lad. You don't want to have anything to do with them." Making a slurping noise, he drank some tea and then leaned further forward towards Jake. "I see something else in your eyes. Not just pride. It's . . . respect for your father. He might've been a daft bugger but . . ." He breathed deeply, trying to control his emotions. "Just don't forget him. And what happened to him."

CHAPTER 10

Grandad Patmore's words echoed in Jake's head like ominous thunder reverberating between valley walls. *They killed your dad, you know*. It was much more his feeling than forensic fact, Jake knew, but he trusted his grandad's instinct. *You don't want to have anything to do with Castleton*. That was tricky. Taken to extremes, it meant that Jake would refuse to have anything to do with his own mother.

Back home, Jake looked down at Tin Can, remembering the robot's hunting capability, and then at his mum. "Could you train TC to zap pigeons?"

When TC was still new to the Patmore household, he'd strutted into the living room, opened his metallic jaw and dropped a dead mouse proudly at Carly's feet.

"Yuck," Jake had said, screwing up his face

"Yeah, but he'll keep the place mouse-free," Carly had replied. "I'll clear it up: Give it a decent burial in the wheelie bin."

"How does he kill them?"

"When he recognises a rat, mouse, cockroach, slug or snail, he zaps them with a laser. If they come close enough to him he can bite and deliver a nasty electric shock at the same time. Stunning. Eat your heart out, Rentokil."

"Will he attack next door's cats by mistake?"

"No. He's programmed to leave the cute and cuddly well alone."

Carly laughed. "That's your grandad talking! Don't you get like him."

Jake told Mum about his visit to Grandad, missing out more than he put in. Then he asked about Grandma Patmore.

Carly sighed. "Sore point. She died soon after your dad was born. Your grandad's always blamed himself. It was a time when he was denying his way with the weather. They were living in York. According to your dad, Grandad could have warned her about torrential rain but he didn't. She went out, walking along the river into town, but she didn't make it back, I'm afraid. No one knows exactly what happened, but there was a flash flood. A bank collapsed, I think. Somehow she slipped over – maybe on the mud – and got washed away." Carly shivered and muttered, "Horrible. And very sad. Your grandad's never really been able to move on."

Jake nodded. No wonder his grandad was a bit nutty. He believed that predicting the weather was dangerous, but Grandma Patmore's accident should have taught him that *not* predicting the weather was just as dangerous. He'd been trapped in a quandary for years.

Grandad's predicament got Jake thinking about all of the Patmores who had come and gone before him. Grandad had referred to Follett Patmore and hinted that he'd come to harm. Yet, in the missing letter, Jake's dad had mentioned an ancestor who was cherished by farmers and travellers for accurate forecasting. Another quandary.

It didn't take Jake long to locate information on Follett Patmore. A website on the history of weather forecasting had two paragraphs on him. In the 17th century, Follett had come up with all sorts of crazy schemes to measure moisture in the air. He'd experimented with anything that expanded or contracted when the air around it got wetter or drier. His crude hygrometers consisted of stretched ox's intestines, human hairs, a rat's bladder, and whalebones. The mad scientist even tied wild oats to dials in an attempt to measure the twisting and untwisting of their sprouts as the humidity changed. It was all too mad for the authorities. Accused of heresy, Follett was locked away.

According to the website, generations of Patmores

had taken an interest in meteorology. Jake had a colour-ful family history. Centuries before Follett, priests were the scientists of their day and they alone could plead with the gods for hospitable weather. Isaac Patmore was a common soothsayer who foretold the weather too well. He was burned to death as a sorcerer because he'd trespassed in an area that belonged to gods and religion.

Jake frowned. Obviously, his dad had omitted the unsavoury bits of the past from his letter. If he'd still been alive, he could have told Jake so much more. It felt strange and sad that Jake was on his own, learning about his family from a cold computer.

Years later, in 1851, two of Follett's descendents had managed to kill themselves in the process of finding out whether air temperature and pressure reduced with height above the ground. The two brothers loaded ther-mometers and barometers into a hot-air balloon and went on a high-altitude journey. Ten kilometres up, they were struck with frostbite and asphyxia. At least their gruesome fate proved their theory.

The computer pinged. It was a sign that another weather chart had arrived from the Midwest via Henson Insurance in London. While Jake studied the details, his frown deepened. Calling Timo Scarpa's mobile, he said, "It's Jake here. Jake Patmore. I got the chart. Can you send me a satellite image of the weather system just west of . . . er . . . Kansas?"

"Why? Have you spotted something already?"

"Maybe. I wish I was there so I could see it and smell it for myself. I bet the locals are staring at a bad-tempered sky."

"I'll sort it out. Land-based or satellite photos, whatever I can get."

"You'd better be quick," Jake replied, "or I'll forecast something after it's all over."

"Right. I'll email you as soon as poss."

It worked out exactly as Jake had feared. Three-quarters of an hour later, when he got more information and predicted a tornado, it was already happening.

"It's a place called Topeka, seventy miles west of Kansas," Timo said by phone. "I'm told it's an F2. There's some damage and injuries in the city but no reports of fatalities yet. Hopefully there won't be any. An F2's strong but not devastating." He paused and then, sounding guilty, added, "I'd better get things moving faster. You need that computer with a direct link to weather satellites. You would've spotted this twister coming if you'd had access to satellite images straight away, wouldn't you?"

"Probably."

"OK. Leave it with me. I'll make it my next job."

"There's something else," Jake said.

"What's that?"

"A trip to Tornado Alley. If I did some storm chasing for a couple of weeks, I'd get a better feel for it."

"Ah." Timo hesitated. "That's awkward. There'd be issues. It's nothing to do with money, but I'd have to speak to your mother. There's school, a visa, making sure you're looked after, safe and supervised, a hundred and one things. But I'll check it out."

In his office at Castleton Computing, Gordon Dell sat at his desk. Elbows tucked into his body, palms outward and open, he said, "Yeah. I know it's difficult. But . . . Let me put it this way. Craig Patmore was good. Yes? Very good. Jake Patmore is better. We can't sit here and watch Henson Insurance wrap him up in contracts. We need him in the Weather-Modification Team now."

"He's fifteen, Gordon," Neisha said.

"Quite right. Where's the problem? Mozart was composing symphonies and touring the world at fourteen. Besides, don't they do work experience at his age?"

Neisha Ray took a deep breath. "Where's the problem? One: he'll hate Castleton because of his dad. Two: Carly won't have it."

Gordon glanced down at the five pages of untidy handwriting and then slipped them into one of his drawers. "You're a friend of the family. You can win them over. That's what I'm paying you for. If you don't deliver him . . ." He shrugged, implying that he'd have to get heavy. Gordon belonged to a new style of management. Dynamic and ruthless. "We know Jake would love to get his hands on his dad's weather model and a supercomputer. Bring him into the WMT and his dream's come true. You'd be doing him a favour. What's Henson doing? They're offering him a Britney Spears CD. We're offering him Britney Spears."

"I don't know about the legal—"

"Let the legal team worry about that," Gordon said, interrupting. "We're not – repeat, not – doing anything wrong. The UN convention on ENMOD isn't a concern. It banned all hostile use of weather modification that causes widespread, long-lasting or severe effects. Note *long-lasting*. We're not doing that. We're triggering a storm, too much rainfall, too little rainfall or whatever, over a short period. Just to get the military edge. The army doesn't want to drop soldiers into the Middle East just before a sandstorm, does it? It wants to wait and let the storm weaken the enemy. Then it sends the troops in while the opposition's still getting sand out of its rifles and digging tanks out of the desert drifts. That's it. No long-term effect. We're onside. Besides, the Government knows what we're doing – it's to their advantage. They'll protect us from an overzealous UN. Anyway, they extracted the UN's teeth over Iraq. We won't get bitten."

"Yes," Neisha replied. "I know all that. I meant, I don't know the employment issues for a boy of fifteen."

"There's no problem. Manchester United sign up promising youngsters all the time. Get on with it, Neisha. Offer him anything. I don't care." Gordon smiled slyly. "Just secure his services for the WMT."

CASTLETON COMPUTING
CONFIDENTIAL

Report, May 2006: Weather-Modification Team

ABSTRACT. Technological advances in meteorology and demands for more precise weather information by multinational businesses and society have led to the identification of the major variables that affect weather. Improvements in computing capability, modelling techniques and atmospheric tracking (mainly through the work of Craig Patmore) have given us an accurate and reliable method for forecasting. The system has been validated against real-world weather.

Current efforts are directed at influencing weather outcomes. This project requires WMT personnel who are experts in both offensive and defensive warfare, and in information and communication technology (ICT). The team also requires a recruit with an indepth understanding of the global weather network and an appreciation of the effects of adding energy or chemicals at particular times. Having assessed all available information on Jake Patmore, we conclude that his skills would enhance the WMT significantly.

INTRODUCTION. Mounting world population

densities are putting pressure on the supply of drinking water and food. At the same time, natural disasters associated with the weather are causing loss of life, property and arable land on an unprecedented scale. Worldwide news coverage is making such disasters increasingly unacceptable. This situation has provoked governments and other organisations into pursuing peaceable environmental modification (ENMOD). Over 20 countries will soon be able to change their local weather patterns by manipulating the factors that result in storms, precipitation or fog. Aims include alleviating drought and deflecting storms from heavily-populated areas. Such civil applications of ENMOD technology also have clear military implications.

Operational Capability	Civil Use	Military Use
Modification of existing storms	(a) Avoidance of hazardous weather (b) Saving life and property damage	(a) Inducing significant enemy casualties (b) Denying enemy operations and movement (c) Inducing lightning strikes on enemy targets, e.g. incapacitating aircraft, causing bushfires to flush out fighters

Creation of storms	None	(a) Inducing significant enemy casualties
		(b) Denying enemy operations and movement
		(c) Inducing lightning strikes on enemy targets, e.g. incapacitating aircraft, causing bushfires to flush out fighters
Enhancement of precipitation	Alleviating water shortages, e.g. reviving withering crops	(a) Flooding lines of communication
		(b) Decreasing morale and comfort level
Denial of precipitation	(a) Reducing flooding	(a) Depriving of fresh water
	(b) Reducing hail damage	(b) Inducing drought
Removal of fog/cloud	Maintaining visibility (now routine at airports)	Denying enemy concealment and reconnoitre
Enhancement of fog/cloud	None	Creating cloud cover to deny enemy visual and infrared surveillance

The modification or creation of storms to support military objectives is the most aggressive and controversial form of weather modification. From a military viewpoint, it is also the most desirable. Storms are capable of inflicting immense damage, both physical and psychological. For example, the energy in a hurricane is equivalent to 10,000 one-megaton hydrogen bombs. While some sections of society and the press will never find weather modification acceptable, we ignore the enormous military benefits of ENMOD at our peril.

CHAPTER 11

Carly looked up from her glass of white wine. "No, Neisha," she said firmly. "Look what happened to Craig."

"What do you mean?" asked Neisha.

"His job really got to him. The stress made him imagine all sorts of conspiracies. But his work was like some sort of addiction. You know, he'd have stood in the path of a tornado if he thought it'd get him more data for his weather model. We all know what that led to." Her eyes went back to the wine glass. "I don't want Jake going down the same road."

"I didn't mean a permanent job or anything. I just happen to know that Gordon would pay a lot. We could all use some extra cash, couldn't we? It'd be like Jake having a paper round and packing supermarket shelves every Saturday morning – but with a lot more kudos. If he wanted to do more, he could check if the school would count it as work experience. And it'd look good on his CV."

The two women were relaxing on opposite sides of the coffee table in Carly's living room. Carly watched her friend taking a gulp of wine, then asked, "Why you, Neisha? Why didn't Gordon call me to his office?"

Neisha smiled. "Come on. He knows we're mates. He thought I'd be more persuasive. If you say no to me, you'll probably get summoned to his lair."

Carly shook her head. "I've just had a chap from Henson Insurance on the line, wanting to whisk Jake off to America for a fortnight. It's spiralling out of control."

"Like a tornado." Grinning, Neisha leaned across and touched Carly's hand. "At least Castleton won't try and take him away. They'll manacle him to the supercomputer. He'll love it and you'll be around to keep an eye on things."

Carly gazed at Neisha and said, "If this was your Erika, what would you do?"

"I'd . . . Well, I'm pretty sure I'd go for it."

"Even if Erika's dad had already come to grief over it?"

"I can't know what that's like, Carly. It's your decision."

Carly threw back her wine. "I need another drink."

Outside school, Aidan was talking to Erika Ray. When Jake joined them, Aidan gave his usual greeting. "Wotcher."

Erika looked at Jake as if she were seeing him for the first time. "Hey," she said brightly.

Jake nodded and smiled. "Hey." He'd always had a crush on Neisha Ray's daughter. There was a time when he thought that his mum and Neisha were trying to push them together deliberately but, like most things forced, it hadn't worked out.

"Still got your head in the clouds? Still a weather nerd?"

Jake looked up at the sky. Hours before, an aeroplane had cruised overhead. Its contrail still hung in the warm humid air and spread outwards to make a band of cirrus. Towards the sun, the thin layers of cloud were coloured in delicate pastel shades by iridescence. "Yes," he said. "It's like the face of a friend."

"Screwy." But Erika made it plain by her expression that she admired him as well.

"*You're* closer to the wind than me."

"How do you mean?"

"Hurricane Erika."

Erika's face lit up. "What? They named a hurricane after me?"

Jake nodded. "At least a couple. One was in 2003. I think it was in the Gulf of Mexico. It wasn't a whopper. Erika was the first big hurricane of the 1997 season, though. It never struck land so it didn't do any great harm."

"Just like me," she replied. "Strong but kind."

Aidan butted in. "Was there a Hurricane Aidan? I bet it kicked ass. I hope so, anyway."

"No. There wasn't a Hurricane Jake either. They recycle the same names every six years. If one gets really notorious – because it kills a lot of people or does a lot of damage – they boot its name into touch and bring on a substitute. Maybe Jake or Aidan will go in next."

"I'm off," Aidan announced in disappointment. "I've got some studio time for mixing." He turned towards Erika and said, "Why don't you come along? I could use a voice like yours."

Erika shook her head. "Another time."

"All right. See you!"

Erika began to stroll along the pavement in the direction of both her own and Jake's house. Clearly, she expected Jake to tag along. "You're a genius at this weather thing. It sounds boring – like, oldies go on about it all the time – but I guess it means you can name your price."

Jake shrugged. "Guess so."

"Mum was talking about it – about you. Castleton would pay you anything – just for an after-school job. Saturday mornings and summer as well, I guess."

"Oh?" Jake felt a twinge of interest, even though Grandad had warned him against the company.

"Rich by the time you leave school. That'd be cool."

"What else did she say?"

"I don't know. Something about a supercomputer and a weather model, whatever that means."

Jake grabbed her arm to stop her walking and then,

embarrassed, let go. "Was she saying I could use them?"

"I think so. Yes. I wasn't paying much attention – well, you don't when your mum's talking, do you? Sounded to me like you'd be working on them. 'All he's got to do is give me the nod and he's in like a shot,' she said. Give *me* the nod and I'll tell her – as long as you pay me back when you're rolling in it."

You don't want to have anything to do with Castleton. They killed your dad, you know.

Jake breathed in deeply. "I'd have to think about that."

"What? Like, if you had a winning lottery ticket, would you have to think about whether to go and claim your millions?"

Jake was in turmoil. He had a sensation in his stomach like the vortex of a tornado. Of course he had to shun Castleton Computing. Stacked against it were a possible murder, Grandad Patmore, and the promotion of weather warfare. But there was something to be said for it as well. Jake thought about stardom, getting his hands on their supercomputer and his dad's mammoth program, and money. Even so, his principles wouldn't let him sign for the company, not after the note from his dad.

"No, I'm not going to . . ."

But, mid-sentence, he was overcome by a thought that came out of nowhere and crashed into his brain like a tidal wave. He could have the best of both worlds. He could lap up the attention, accept the riches, *and* keep his principles. He could take the job but, while he was working for Castleton, he could investigate his father's suspicions and his grandad's accusation. He'd be a mole – a double agent.

"You're crazy," Erika was saying, shaking her head in dismay.

"Yeah. I suppose you've got a point."

Surprised by the sudden change of mind, Erika became chirpy again. "So, I'll tell Mum you'll give it a go?"

"If you like, but . . ."

"What?"

"Well, there's Mum," said Jake.

"Hmm. She won't have it?"

"I doubt it."

"You never know till you try. If it's a problem, my mum could get her drunk. That way, I bet she'll agree."

Jake hesitated, then asked, "Why are you doing this, Erika?"

"I'm your friend, aren't I? Friends are supposed to help each other out."

CHAPTER 12

Jake detected the smell of alcohol on his mum. She was sozzled. It wasn't a spectacular loss of control – she didn't burst into song or dance on the dining table. But she opened up. And out poured her worries.

"You're a soldier, Jake. You've been posted by an oil pipeline and told to defend it against terrorists by shooting to kill. Think about it. You see a woman with a pram coming towards you. What do you do?"

"Nothing."

"Mmm. Even though she could be a suicide bomber with a pram stuffed full of explosives?"

Jake nodded. "She could have a pram stuffed full of babies."

"All right. Now you see a man coming towards you. He's clutching something to his chest. It could be a child or it could be a missile launcher under a blanket."

"I still don't shoot."

"But that's not what your orders say. If he's going to blow up the pipeline, you've got to shoot – maybe even straight through his baby – to kill him."

"No. You said *if* he's going to attack the pipeline. Until I know he's up to no good, I'm doing nothing."

"OK. Let's say he's a known terrorist."

Jake sighed. "I still wouldn't shoot in case he's got a baby. It's only a pipeline."

"So, you disobey your orders."

"Yes."

"Your conscience comes first."

"I guess so."

"Right," his mum said. "Now think about a robot. No conscience, but the same orders. Shoot anyone who looks like they're going to blow up the pipeline. We're not talking Terminator here. It's not Arnie striding up and down. It's probably something more like TC, with wheels for better mobility, sensors for seeing, and a gun. Here comes that mum and pram again. First problem. Will its sensors see a mother and pram or will it think it's a terrorist pushing a gun carriage or something? I think I've cracked that one." She hesitated to let out a loud hiccup. "Our robot soldiers should recognise a mother pushing a pram. Just. But the robot still doesn't know what's in the pram. What does it do?"

"It shouldn't shoot."

"But it's not worrying about feeling guilty. The easiest thing for it to do is to fire – just in case. It'll secure the oil supply or it'll kill a mother and child. It won't lose sleep either way. It won't sleep at all."

"You've got to program it to identify danger before it'll open fire."

"Easier said than done," his mum replied. "What's dangerous? Maybe the pram. And if the robot's programmed to do nothing when a child's in the firing line, all the bad guys will learn to take children on their missions." Barely stopping to take a breath, she continued, "Now, that man's heading your way with a baby or some sort of weapon under a blanket. Is that dangerous enough to shoot?"

"I don't know," Jake answered.

"No. Neither does the robot. That's what I'm working on. It's tough for a machine to spot the difference between a child, a bomb, and a rifle if they're wrapped in someone's arms. And the robot can't phone a friend. It's got its orders and no conscience."

Her eyes were raw, heavy and alert in turn. Tin Can the copycat was struggling to keep pace with her moods. He settled on restless anxiety and prowled around on legs that were wobbly at the best of times.

Jake was stunned by his mum's revelations. He had no idea that her work had gone so far. Dismayed, he asked, "Why do you do this job, Mum?"

"Castleton started out with toys and domestic robots and now it's into defence." She shrugged. "If I didn't do it, someone else would. And I keep thinking someone else might not be as eager as me to get the artificial intelligence right. I'd rather be improving the automatic lawn mower or making a toy but, right now, I'm working hard on the decision-making. The robot won't have a conscience so I'm putting as much of mine into the programming as I can. I want it as humane as possible. You see, I approve. Deploying robots will stop human soldiers getting butchered. I just don't want my robots killing innocent people. I want to be able to sleep at night."

It was like the weather, Jake thought. That didn't have a conscience either. It didn't feel pity or remorse. Nature's assassin used storms, heat waves, floods and droughts to destroy and damage without a thought, without a heart. True, its sunlight and rain nourish the planet, but the weather didn't care one way or the other about life or death. And this particular mass murderer didn't recognise boundaries, either. Turned loose in one country, a storm couldn't be recalled or disabled. It would go where it pleased and it would have knock-on effects around the globe. Jake hoped that robot soldiers would be different.

"Your robots. You must be able to work out where they are. Can you blow them up if they get out of hand?"

Carly nodded. "They're called ABUs – autonomous battlefield units. They're tuned into the global positioning system so they won't get lost. And if things go wrong . . . well, they don't volunteer for self-destruction – they're not suicidal – but they've got human operators – minders – who've got their fingers on the button. They can be disabled at a distance. Their innards are incinerated completely so the enemy can't get its hands on a live one."

Jake had another thought. A nasty thought. If ABUs replaced soldiers so that equipment got pulverised rather than troops, wars would be too easy to wage. They'd become acceptable because only the enemy would suffer casualties. The whole thing saddened him immensely. He wished all this clever technology was used to help people, not to kill them. That's what his dad would have thought as well. Jake recalled a couple of sentences from his dad's letter. *I developed this computer model as the first step to preventing the misery, damage and death that extreme weather can bring. I didn't do it so storms could be aimed at people on purpose.* The sooner Jake became a Castleton Computing mole, the better.

"Mum. I want to work at Castleton as well. A bit now and over the summer."

"I know." She put her hand over her mouth while something between a hiccup and a burp emerged.

Deciding his best chance was to tackle her while she was drunk, he threw caution to the winds. "You work there. Why shouldn't I?"

She shrugged. "I don't know. Put like that, I don't suppose I've got a leg to stand on. I just don't want you to get obsessive about it."

"Are you saying I can?"

"Subject to some reassurances about homework. But don't get the idea I'm happy about it. I'm not. Nowhere near happy."

"Thanks, Mum."

"Yeah," she muttered. "I'll tell you one thing, though. It's weird to think we might end up working together. I program unmanned planes for spying and gathering data. They go out to all sorts of inaccessible places and beam weather information back. The data goes into your dad's computer model."

Jake nodded and said, "Keeping it in the family. I wonder what he would have made of it all."

Immediately, his mum looked sober, but she didn't reply.

Occupying a corner of the carefully air-conditioned room were four large stacks of processors. In the centre were two workstations, on opposite sides of a rectangle of desks. On the other side of the room there were two massive laser printers. One of the monitors was adorned with a colourful radar image of a live gale in the North Sea. On the wall, there was a notice.

The flap of a butterfly's wing in Brazil
can set off a tornado in Texas.
Edward Lorenz, Professor of Meteorology, MIT.

"Have you ever seen anything like this?" asked Gordon Dell.

Jake shook his head. He felt like a child let loose in a toy factory. "This is what Dad worked on?" he asked.

"The very same. The best weather model in the world – by a mile."

Jake reckoned there'd be plenty of time later to remind himself that he was a deeply suspicious undercover agent. Right now, he just wanted to marvel at it all. "What do you want me to do?"

"First, you're going to learn how to use the program," Gordon replied. "Get a feel for what it can do before we get a feel for what you can do." He spread out his arms. "Play with it. It's all yours – with a bit of supervision."

Supervision came in the shape of Brian Mosby. The bright-eyed leader of the Weather-Modification Team said, "I have to tell you, I'm a huge admirer of your dad. His model's a fantastic achievement. It gives near-perfect three-day forecasts and it's pretty reliable up to ten days ahead. It takes every single detail of today's weather conditions and then works out exactly what the five million billion tonnes of air over our heads will do. That's an unbelievably complex calculation."

Plainly, Brian was super-enthusiastic about the supercomputer. He was a small man with big glasses but he didn't look geeky. He was too elegant to be a geek. His hairstyle, his smart clothes; everything was expensive. Even his deodorant smelled expensive.

"How does it work?" asked Jake.

"Sit down," Brian said, grabbing a second chair for himself and parking it in front of a monitor. "Above us, we've got a fickle layer of gas – the atmosphere, fifty miles thick – powered by colossal amounts of energy from the sun. Mathematically, you can't treat it as one big bubble. It's just too complicated. Your dad broke it down into manageable chunks – bite-size boxes of weather, if you like, ten kilometres across. Each box acts in sync with its neighbouring boxes. The computer stores data on the weather in every box. It projects into the future by just a few minutes, calculating where the weather in each box will go and how it'll change. It's a supercomputer so it does hundreds of billions of calculations every second. Then it does it again, working out what happens in each box a few minutes later. And again and again. All the while it's getting updates on real worldwide weather conditions and refining its starting point. It keeps doing that till it's looking at tomorrow's pattern. Then it produces charts that define tomorrow's weather." Brian rested a hand on the terminal like a lover touching his partner. "Given more computing time, it can look further forward, up to about ten days. But the further ahead you push it, the more computer time you need and the fuzzier it gets."

"So, it's predicting the weather right round the globe, not just here."

"If you want an outlook for Tuvalu, we've got it – courtesy of your dad. If only he were still . . ." Brian looked at Jake and said, "Sorry. But he was a great man. Such a pity the world lost him. He'd be doing brilliant work."

"Did you know him?"

"Not in the way you mean. But I think I do, yes. He left so much of himself in here." He tapped the top of the terminal. "I think I know him pretty well."

Jake nodded.

"Come on," Brian said eagerly. "You don't want to sit here listening to me talk. You want to tee off. But before we can train *you*, you've got to train the computer."

"How do you mean?"

"It's your mum's idea. A security device. You log on to the computer with a user name, but there's no password. Instead there's voice-recognition software. You've got to say your name loud and clear, and then the date and time. If it all checks out, the computer lets you into all those parts that you're cleared for. So," Brian said, "you need to say your name now – ten times, I'm afraid. The system archives your voice for matching in the future. In your first week here, it listens and trains itself to recognise the way you talk so it knows it's you when you say the date and time." He glanced at Jake and added, "If I had to log on now, I'd read the time from the screen and say, 'Brian H Mosby, Monday twelfth of June, two thousand and six, sixteen forty-three.'"

"Right."

"Come on. Let's get it over with, then we can get into the good stuff: weather model, lesson one."

CHAPTER 13

Aidan's right arm was hanging casually from one of the pegs in the cloakroom area just off the main school corridor. "If you ask me, you're better off without a dad. Mine's a pain. He's got one simple philosophy. Football – manly. Music – girly. That's it. Not what you'd call deep. Still, as least I've got a break from matches till next season."

School had finished for the day. Soon, Aidan would make his way to the sound studio to mix some more tracks on a computer. Jake would make his way to Castleton Computing to mix atmospheric conditions on a supercomputer. Both of them would feel like pilots in control of their individual aeroplanes.

"Yeah, but it'd be different for me," Jake replied. "Me and Dad would like the same things."

"You only think that because he's not around."

"No. Because of his letter."

Aidan nodded. "The famous disappearing letter. That's really got to you, hasn't it?"

"Yes," Jake admitted.

"I know you're hacked off that it's gone, but you did

98

read it, didn't you? It's not like you don't know what he said."

"Yeah, but . . ." Jake shook his head and propped himself against a stand. "It's a bit of my dad – the only bit that's mine – and someone's nicked it. They shouldn't have. I reckon he went to a lot of bother to write it for me and now . . ."

"Well, who knew about it?"

"Me and the solicitor. Oh. And Grandad, but that was after it'd gone. He blames Castleton."

"Why? How could they take it?"

Jake shrugged. "I'm going to try and find out."

On the other side of the coat rack, Erika Ray chirped, "Hey. What are you two talking about?"

"Nothing," Jake answered.

She came round the end, collected her coat and sidled up to the boys. "Please yourselves." She thumped Jake's shoulder playfully. "I got you that job."

"Yeah. Sort of. Thanks."

Cosmic Cosgrove was the next to interrupt. Heading down the corridor towards the staff room, he paused and said in his Geordie accent, "How there. What's this about a job?"

"It's all kosher, sir," Erika replied. "Honest."

"What is?"

Erika answered, "Jake's got a job at Castleton – like my mum, but doing weather stuff."

Cosmic gazed at Jake. "Is that right?"

99

Jake nodded.

The Geography teacher looked impressed. "You're a canny lad. Some other time, you'll have to tell me all about it. I'm interested. Very interested."

"OK."

Cosmic was about to go but he hesitated. "I'm doing a field trip in the Peaks with the little 'uns next week, Jake. Tuesday. Any good?"

Jake sucked in air through his teeth and shook his head. "You'll need wet-weather gear."

"Damn. Pity you can't change it for me. Anyway, thanks."

On the way to Castleton Computing, with Erika walking beside him, Jake made up his mind. He turned to her and said, "Has your mum mentioned a letter in the last month?"

"A letter? What sort of letter?"

Jake knew he was sailing close to the wind, but he continued anyway. "Something to do with me, Castleton, and my dad, Craig."

Erika thought about it for a moment and then said, "Don't think so. I'll ask her about it, if you like."

"No!" Jake snapped.

"All right. No need to yell."

"Sorry. Just forget it. I didn't even ask." He glanced at her and, as always, felt a slight quickening of his heart. It meant he still fancied her.

Erika shrugged and pointed to the newsagent's. "The chocolate's on you. You owe me that."

"I'm still only getting pocket money."

"What's happening to your billions?"

"Mum's setting up some sort of trust – whatever that means – so I get it when I'm eighteen."

Erika shook her head. "Sorry, I can't wait that long. I'm hungry. Come on." She took his arm and dragged him towards the shop.

Timo Scarpa's gift arrived in four huge cardboard boxes. Courtesy of Henson Insurance, the package included a man in a van. At the cost of a coffee and two chocolate biscuits, he rigged up the satellite dish, installed the decoder and set up everything. Jake didn't have to do a thing – except predict tornadoes.

It was great for Jake to have his own home computer, yet he couldn't help comparing it with the system at Castleton. The PC in his bedroom had a good range of weather software but it was krill to Castleton's whale. Still, Jake appreciated it and everything it implied. It meant that people thought he was special. He loved being pampered for his meteorological flair. He welcomed the attention of both Henson Insurance and Castleton Computing, even if their motives were more financial than charitable.

His PC had access to satellite data but it left the

crunching of large collections of numbers to mega-computers in weather stations all around the world and received their reports. Its software built new weather maps every three hours for surface conditions. Every twelve hours, it updated the charts with upper-air observations from the 1,500 weather balloons released each day to measure temperature, moisture and pressure up to an altitude of 30 kilometres.

Two days after its installation, Jake spotted trouble brewing in Tennessee. A geostationary satellite parked 36,000 kilometres above America was taking pictures of cloud formations with visible light and infrared radiation.

Telephoning Timo, Jake said, "You've got a storm brewing in Jackson, Tennessee. It'll produce tornadoes tomorrow."

"What? Tomorrow? You can see that far ahead?"

"The wind'll blow in two different directions at the same time. There'll be warm air underneath trying to rise up through the cold air mass above. Perfect for tornadoes. But they might be tiddlers. I don't know yet. I'll keep an eye on it and give you a call if I can tell how big they're going to be. I'll check it on a weather model as well."

"Oh? Which?" asked Timo.

"I'm not sure I should say, but I'm working part-time at Castleton Computing."

There were a few seconds of silence before Timo said,

"You mean, you can run it through your dad's super-computer?"

"Yes. Is that all right?"

"All right? It's brilliant."

Robert Goodhart had a different attitude. He arrived unannounced at Jake's house in the evening and got straight down to business. "Timo tells me you've got access to Castleton's weather model."

Jake nodded. "It's amazing."

"Yes. It's great for Timo – and for you. I wish I could play with it as well. But there's a problem, Jake. I'm sorry, but it's ruined our research. I'm going to have to back out halfway through. No more testing."

"Why?"

Robert smiled kindly at him. "It's all about integrity and perception. You see, I was testing *you*. Yes? Not a machine. You've got to look at it from my point of view – from a scientific point of view. I'd be measuring your ability to forecast the weather at the same time that you're using a supercomputer-based weather model. It'd be like testing you on mental arithmetic while you're holding a calculator. If you do brilliantly well – which I know you will – the outside world will think you used the computer. I know you wouldn't cheat—"

Jake interrupted. "No, I wouldn't."

"But outsiders'll never be convinced because you

had the *opportunity* to cheat. Science won't tolerate results that aren't foolproof. And, I admit, I've got to think about my own credibility."

"But . . ."

"Even if you and I could persuade everyone that you haven't deliberately cheated, it's hard – impossible – to argue that you're not influenced subconsciously by the supercomputer's forecasts."

Jake sighed, but he also nodded. He understood. When he thought about it, though, he realised that Dr Goodhart's withdrawal wasn't such a big thing. The main reason he'd wanted to be tested was to prove he was accurate enough to get a job in weather prediction. At the age of fifteen, he'd already got two jobs. This particular cloud, Jake thought, had a silver lining.

CHAPTER 14

IN A SPIN
Tornadoes

*Tornadoes have the fastest air on Earth: up to 300 mph,
maybe more. No wind-measuring gear has ever survived an encounter with a violent tornado. Remote
radar recorded a top speed of 318 mph for an Oklahoma
tornado in 1999. Tornadoes are erratic storms: they can
last for seconds or hang around for three hours; they are
as narrow as a road or as wide as a town; they travel a
few metres or several miles in straight lines, curves or
even circles. They are usually funnel-shaped and they
have levelled whole towns and forests. The low air pressure inside them has exploded houses and mobile homes,
plucked chickens, thrown trains off their tracks, pulled
the wings off aircraft, picked up a house and turned it
90 degrees before setting it back down sideways to the
street, wrenched asphalt from roads, carried a spire 20
miles away from its church, sucked up and then spat out
people, cars and animals.*

*3 May 1999: A mile-wide tornado, spinning at well
over 200 mph, ripped through 38 miles of Oklahoma*

*26th September 1971: a tornado shoved a 90-ton
train 50 metres along the railway track in Rotherham,
Yorkshire.*

In the next couple of hours, Jackson would fall silent.
People and pets would take to tornado shelters. The
streets would be eerily empty and all the birds would
fly away. Then, a finger of cloud would jab viciously at
the ground and spin like water going down a drain. Its
extraordinary noise – louder than an onrushing train –
would obliterate all other sound.

"Are you sure?" asked Timo, his voice grim.

"Yes. I can see it. Dad's model can see it. I'm looking
at the satellite photo now. There'll be at least one big
tornado, close to Jackson."

"It's a hell of a thing to send people scurrying to their
storm shelters or even evacuating them completely."

"What can I say?" Jake muttered. "It's an ugly brute
of a storm. I can see it developing all over my nice new
monitor."

"Yes. The National Weather Service is monitoring it
as well. They'll only issue a warning when someone
sees it touching the ground."

"That could be too late for some."

"If you give people false warnings," Timo said, "they
don't take any notice next time. That's when it becomes

life or death. I'll tell you what happens, Jake. I've seen it in Dallas. There's nothing on Earth as frightening and unstoppable as a big tornado. It growls like constant thunder. I saw an F4 tornado pick a car up with a woman inside and smash it through the brick wall of a house. It ended up in the second-storey bedroom – wrecked. The woman survived but her ribs and hips were shattered. People get yanked out of their homes. Ones that survive say they've seen cars, cows and rocks spinning around them. It's like being in a spin drier with a load of stones. Terrifying. What kills them isn't the wind. It's all the stuff that gets hoovered up with them. A tornado turns stones into bullets. Road signs, tiles and furniture all become high-velocity missiles. Broken glass thrashes around like flying blades. It's sliced arms and legs off. One girl was almost cut in half. And the worst thing – at speed, dust and mud kill people by sandblasting skin from their bodies. A violent twister's the smart missile of the weather world."

Jake noted that his dad wasn't the only one who compared the weather with weapons. "Sounds to me like a good reason to warn everyone."

"I'm just trying to weigh your confidence against lost credibility if you get it wrong."

"I'm as sure as I can be."

"All right," Timo replied, sighing heavily. "I'll talk to my colleagues in America."

"Before you do . . ."

107

"Yes?"

"You know that trip to Tornado Alley?"

"I'm struggling . . ."

"No need," Jake said. "Forget it. I'm too busy now."

At last, Timo allowed himself a little laugh. "You sound like a businessman all of a sudden." He paused and then added, "I'll let you know about Jackson."

CHAPTER 15

Castleton Computing reached for the sky. The building didn't occupy much ground. Instead, it rose upwards. The weather laboratory was on the top floor, underneath the air-conditioning unit on the flat roof. The room was a spacious cockpit that bore Craig Patmore's signature everywhere. It was kept immaculately clean and organised. Jake Patmore sat inside it and felt close to his father – the ghost in the machine. As the other bond between them – his dad's letter – had vanished into thin air, the weather machine would have to suffice.

Jake was waiting at one of workstations while, opposite him, Brian tinkered with the other. The scene resembled an electronic game with the two opponents facing each other across a computer desk. Or maybe they were colleagues about to take on a sinister threat to the world. Eventually Jake's supervisor looked at him and said, "Are you ready?"

Jake was about to learn why Brian Mosby led a group called the Weather-Modification Team rather than the Weather-Prediction Team. He nodded.

"OK. I'm going to give you weather charts for East China and Korea. They're not real. Have you heard of a flight simulator? You know, when a pilot trains on something that looks and feels like a real plane, but isn't?"

"I think so."

"Well, that's what I've done with the weather. I'm running a simulation. It's one with a typhoon blowing up the East China Sea, over the Yellow Sea, heading straight for South Korea."

"I see it," Jake said, staring at the same pattern on the monitor in front of him. "What do you want to me to do? Predict where the typhoon's going to hit?"

"No. I'll tell you that for free. It's going to strike Inchon, on the coast near Seoul. Got it?"

"Yes."

"This is more about altering than forecasting. Inchon's heavily populated. A typhoon would do a lot of damage. But it's a big step between predicting the weather and modifying or mastering it. Craig – I mean, your dad – got as far as programming the system to tell us what would happen if someone seeded rainfall in one particular box. He also got it to work out what you'd need to modify a gale. I want you to modify this storm. It sounds tough but typhoons and hurricanes are about the easiest to tackle. So many meteorologists have studied them for so long, they're our best-understood weather system. We know hurricanes inside out. The ball's lying nicely in the open."

"Sorry?"

"We want to swing the storm away from the town. You could aim for an unpopulated region or keep it from landfall altogether."

"Why me? Can't the computer do it? Sounds like Dad's programming could take care of it."

"Yes, but there's a problem. It makes up a lot of different scenarios and runs calculations on each one to find out what effect they have, searching for the smallest shunt that would send a hurricane where we want it to go. But it's a huge job. By the time the processors have crunched countless calculations and worked out the best way of altering the storm's path, it's already struck land. You might say it makes heavy weather of the job. We need someone to narrow the options down – to figure out what sort of tweak in which box is most likely to work. That way, we'd cut computing time down to something reasonable, something practical. That's where you come in."

Jake nodded. "That's why you told me all that stuff about hurricanes yesterday."

"Do you remember it?" Brian asked, like a schoolteacher.

"A hurricane's attracted to warmth. Like a magnet, you said. Dad's model reckons that strong warming could knock a hurricane off course by a hundred kilometres or so."

"Exactly. But a computer doesn't have a feel for the

weather – not even your dad's. It just calculates whatever you ask it to calculate. We don't know where to tell it to begin. Think of a game of chess on a huge three-dimensional board with millions of pieces. The computer can calculate all possible moves to win the game, but it would take years. We need someone to identify the key pieces and give us an idea where to move them to. A lad finely tuned to the weather would do the job. What's this typhoon going to do if you could warm a mass of air somewhere near it?"

"But you can't, can you?"

Brian smiled at him and shrugged. "It doesn't matter. It's just theoretical. It'll feel real enough when you fine-tune the weather system on screen and see what the effect is, but the storm only exists in the computer. The typhoon's made up, so you can make up anything you think will persuade it to swerve away from Inchon. You don't have to worry about making it realistic."

"But—"

Brian interrupted Jake's objection. "All right. Let's say, I could envisage planes warming the air above an ocean with specially-adapted microwave heaters."

"But it's fantasy, isn't it? You can't actually do it."

"That's right."

"OK. Let me have a think about it. I haven't done anything like this before." Jake began to study the isobars, the wind direction at different heights, the upper-air contours, the temperatures.

"No hurry," said Brian. "Take your time."

First, Jake ran the program to track the ominous whirl of cumulus and cumulonimbus as it skimmed over the Yellow Sea, feeding on the warm ocean water and whipping up the waves, until it crashed into Inchon. While he watched the accelerated sequence, many times faster than a real typhoon's speed, he thought of Typhoon Nina and his dad. He wondered if his dad had programmed this artificial storm or whether it was Brian's creation. Perhaps it was based on the real Nina, which ravaged the nearby Chinese coast thirty-one years ago.

Jake looked up and asked, "Has this typhoon got a name?"

"It has now," Brian answered. "Typhoon Jake. In South Korea – particularly Pusan harbour – they get battered a lot. They copped Maemi three years ago. A hundred people dead and twenty-five thousand homeless when the wind got up to a hundred and thirty miles an hour. A typhoon's called 'evil wind spirit' there."

Something told Jake that he wanted to send the typhoon further north – to the border between South Korea and North Korea where he could not see any towns. He created a hot spot just to the northwest of Inchon where part of China and North Korea reached out for each other across the Yellow Sea. He hoped it would attract the typhoon but, when he ran the sequence again, the path of Typhoon Jake was not noticeably different. The population of Inchon still got a pretend pounding and drenching.

Of course, that made sense. It was silly to try and alter the storm's direction when it was so close to landfall. He needed to nudge it when it was a long way off the shore.

Jake was reminded of a disaster movie about a giant asteroid hurtling through space towards Earth. It was so enormous that a prod close to impact wouldn't save Earth from a catastrophic collision. But the same small prod applied when the asteroid was much further away would change the speed and angle of its flight slightly. At first, the tiny deflection would be barely perceptible but, as the asteroid crossed the millions of miles on its journey towards Earth, the nudge would be enough to send it wide of the planet.

He examined the map again. He had a gut feeling that warm air off Shanghai would make the evil wind spirit veer to the west as it passed between China and Japan. He ran the storm sequence in reverse, sending the typhoon back to its roots in the Pacific Ocean, just beyond the line of Ryukyu Islands. In his mind, he tried to imagine what would happen to the weather map if he warmed some of the boxes between Taiwan and Shanghai. He made his choice intuitively, heated the air by five degrees, and ran the program again.

Tracking the typhoon, Jake smiled as it departed

slightly from its original path. It was veering to the northwest, but not by much. Instead of slamming into south Inchon, it hit land in the north of the city. Jake's smile dissipated like fog in warmth and wind.

Across the desk, Brian cried, "That's fantastic. Second attempt and you shifted it about ten miles!"

"Not enough," Jake replied grimly.

"The computer might have tied itself up in calculations for a day to get a result like that."

Jake shrugged. "I'll move it a lot more this time," he said, choosing a different collection of boxes further out into the East China Sea.

The third sequence took them both by surprise. Typhoon Jake swerved westerly and bypassed Inchon altogether.

Jake looked across at Brian with a smug smile. His way with the weather and his dad's programming skills made quite a partnership. "It's a breeze," Jake joked.

The storm appeared to move more slowly this time because the supercomputer was labouring to work out an entirely new trajectory for it. On the monitors, the mass of spiralling cloud headed into Korea Bay.

Brian and Jake were transfixed, both watching the same graphics but on their separate screens. Brian said excitedly, "It's going to hit Korea higher up. North Korea."

Realising before Brian what he'd done, Jake was

dismayed. Suddenly, he felt very uncomfortable. "It's going to hit Pyongyang instead," Jake muttered.

He was right. The typhoon swung towards land and smashed into North Korea's sprawling capital city.

Brian didn't appear to mind. He still seemed to think the experiment was a major triumph. He was thrilled. "That's absolutely brilliant," he said, jumping up. "Hole in one."

"But . . ."

"Don't worry about it. It's all make-believe." Elated, Brian laughed and added, "Anyway, it's much better to hit North Korea than South, politically speaking. Axis of evil and all that." He strode towards the door, saying, "Wait here. I've got to tell Gordon."

Alone in the room, Jake thought of Robert Goodhart. The university scientist would not have allowed himself to get carried away after one experiment. He'd be warning Jake that it could have been a fluke. A one-off. He'd be asking Jake to repeat the exercise with a different storm in a different part of the globe. And, if he was successful again, he'd have to prove himself for a third and a fourth time. Then, maybe, Robert would start to believe that Jake had a talent for it. But he'd still hold back because he hadn't demonstrated that a real storm in the real world would react in the same way.

Jake wondered also about the knock-on effects of what he had done. He was well aware that changing the conditions in one area would change it everywhere else because the weather in neighbouring parts of the planet was closely coupled. His eye caught the poster on the wall again.

*The flap of a butterfly's wing in Brazil can
set off a tornado in Texas.*

He might lure a hurricane away from Belize and, as a result, cause a deluge over the Caribbean. Saving Belize could be a catastrophe for farmers, islanders and tourists in vulnerable Caribbean Islands. Still, Jake was comforted by the fact that Castleton didn't have the technology to increase the temperature of a large air mass. No one had it. And, besides, the typhoon was not real.

He got up to stretch his legs and noticed for the first time that there was a grey folder on Brian's part of the desk. Drawn to it, Jake glanced at its cover.

CASTLETON COMPUTING
CONFIDENTIAL
Report, May 2006: Weather-Modification Team

Well, Jake was part of the WMT now. He'd just shown them that he was a vital part of the team. Looking around furtively, he opened the file and read.

METHODS AND DISCUSSION. Technologically, we must have a firm understanding of the variables that affect the weather. We must be able to model the dynamics of their interactions, map their possible outcomes, measure their real-time values, and influence them to achieve a desired result.

The main requirement for weather modification is a proven set of intervention techniques. The number of intervention methods is limited only by our imagination but, with few exceptions, they involve introducing either energy or chemicals into the atmosphere at the right place and time, and in the right form. The intervention would be designed to alter the weather in several ways, e.g. changing cloud cover and precipitation, the intensity and direction of storms, conditions in space, or fog.

Proven methodologies. (a) Particles of sulphates and nitrates reduce droplet size in clouds, inhibiting rainfall and snowfall. This may be a way of inducing droughts. (b) Cloud seeding causes a developing thunderstorm to strengthen over a given target, significantly restricting the enemy's ability to manoeuvre and defend themselves. (c) Microwave heating disperses fog and disrupts radar systems.

Developing methodologies. (a) Thousands of airborne robotic specks (nanorobots) communicating with each other may be used to produce artificial clouds at will. (b) Atmospheric manipulation (mainly heating) may create storms and redirect hurricanes. With weather satellites CC3 and CC4 in place, an effective method for targeted atmospheric heating—

The door opened and Jake slammed the file shut. Trying not to look guilty, he turned to face Gordon Dell, Neisha Ray and Brian Mosby.

The door opened and Jake slammed the folder shut. He took no notice of his new bodyguard who came into the room.

CHAPTER 16

It was a fine Friday afternoon, late in June. High above Castleton's tall building, five white clouds looked like commas in a line. They were altocumulus with watery tails. Ice particles fell vertically from each cloud, until they melted into water droplets. Then, the droplets began to evaporate and fall more slowly, leaving a bent fallstreak behind the main cloud as the wind blew it sedately across the sky. From a different angle, the clouds looked like a line of skydiving jellyfish. The water in the fallstreaks dispersed into vapour well before reaching the ground so they didn't produce rain.

Gordon glanced at the folder and then gazed into Jake's face. With a grin, he said, "I hear our secret ingredient's come up trumps. You've started to earn your wages already."

Jake nodded but said nothing in case his voice quaked after his first bit of spying on Gordon Dell's business.

"Time I had words with your school," Gordon continued. "We need you here more, maybe on work

120

experience. That'd be good, wouldn't it? We need you to shift lots of storms while Brian programs the computer to learn from what you do. Then we're closer to made-to-measure weather. If we go one step further and understand how you do it . . . well, the sky's the limit. Actually, near-space is the limit. Just think of the lives and properties we'd save."

"That's why you're doing it, is it?" Jake dared to ask.

"Quite right," Gordon replied.

Jake didn't really expect the manager to admit to military uses, even if they were uppermost in his mind. "You still couldn't alter the weather. You'd know how to do it, if you could heat great chunks of air. But you can't."

"You're part of Castleton now, Jake. It's not a matter of, '*You* can't do this or that.' It's 'we'."

"OK. *We* can't heat up a particular bit of the atmosphere."

Gordon's expression did not change. His smooth face didn't reveal disappointment or denial. "We have several other research projects." His eyes drifted down to the grey folder again before he added, "If you want to know anything going on in the company, just ask Neisha. She'll be happy to tell you all you want to know."

Jake glanced at his mum's friend. He got the impression that Neisha would be happy to tell him everything the company wanted him to know. "Thanks," he

121

muttered, turning back to Gordon. "Can I bring my camera in and get a few shots of Dad's supercomputer?"

"No," Gordon answered. "We don't allow cameras on site – for security reasons. It's in your employment contract." He sat beside one of the screens and said, "Show me what you did, Jake. Impress me."

"How does it feel to be a hero?" Timo said, clearly on a high.

Jake hesitated. He'd been so absorbed by his feat at Castleton that he'd almost forgotten his prediction of a Tennessee twister. "Jackson got its tornado, then?"

"Two."

"What happened?"

On the other end of the phone, Timo answered, "Power cables and telephone lines came down. A few trailers – mobile homes anchored on concrete – got wrecked. Some houses and cars were damaged, but no one got hurt. Not a single person. They were in shelters. A boy, sitting in front of his computer thousands of miles away in Britain, gave the first warning in plenty of time. Amazing. If the people of Jackson knew your name, they'd have it up in lights by now."

"What about Henson Insurance?"

"The payout's going to be piffling. No claims for injury or death."

It made Jake feel good. A weather prophet's duty was to save people. That's what he wanted to do. At

Castleton, he felt tossed between pride and his principles. He liked to flaunt his uncanny skill but he wouldn't help the company convert the weather into a weapon, if that was Castleton's aim. In his dad's words, he wouldn't become a prized soldier. That was well beyond his comfort zone.

Timo added, "I'm sending you a token of our appreciation. And I'll be in touch. You'll keep your eyes open for anything else, won't you?"

"I am already. Some thunderstorms are brewing in the Atlantic off west Africa. They're no problem at the moment, but I've got a hunch. Satellite radar says the ocean's a lot warmer there than normal. That's extra fuel for the storms. If they merge, they'll make a giant and head towards America."

"OK. Better keep me posted. Have a good weekend."

Jake put the phone down and looked at TC. The pretend pooch was looking pleased with himself, like an old dog that had just learned a new trick. "I'm one of the universe's great mysteries, you know. Mum said so. And I've just saved a whole batch of people in Tennessee. Dad would be proud of me, I reckon." Jake bent down and stroked the contact sensors on the top of TC's smooth head. "There's something I don't understand, though. If Dad sabotaged his own supercomputer, he didn't do it very well, did he? Maybe he had his accident – or whatever it was – before he got a chance to pull the plug. Or maybe he killed it off but the company's resurrected it. Maybe Brian Mosby repaired the damage. I don't know."

Distracted, Jake gazed out of his bedroom window. Grey shading made the white middle-level clouds look like a honeycomb. Well on its way to the western horizon, the sun was shining through a thin, round hole in the altocumulus.

"There's one thing I *do* know," he told TC. "I've got to get deeper into the programming. I'm worried . . . It was something about the way that typhoon hit North Korea. I know it wasn't real. Even so . . . Then there's that report. It talked about making droughts and ways of heating the atmosphere. It was going to say something about satellites CC3 and CC4. I wish I'd . . . but Gordon Dell came in. He didn't answer my question about messing around with real hurricanes, but he didn't deny it."

The doorbell interrupted. Leaning on the banister at the top of the landing, Jake watched his mum open the door to Neisha and Erika Ray. He was surprised. It was ages since Erika had dropped in with her mum. Jake knew why Neisha would visit on a Friday night – to share gossip and white wine with his mum – but why Erika?

He went back into his bedroom and waited while TC made his way painfully slowly down the stairs.

Erika must have passed the mechanical mongrel mid-flight because she knocked on Jake's door, came in and then looked back, cooing, "Hey, he's cute."

Jake pretended that he didn't know what she was talking about. "Who?"

"Your robot dog. Oh. He's changed his mind, he's coming back up."

"He checks strangers out. He's probably recognised your mum's voice as the usual harmless visitor. Perhaps he's not so sure about you. If you're going to murder me, you'd better do it quickly – before he comes back in." To change the subject, Jake asked, "Have you still got that pet rat?"

"Chewy? Yeah. She's cute as well – with the added advantage that she scares people." Suddenly distracted, Erika looked beyond Jake. "Wow! State-of-the-art!"

Jake followed her gaze to his new computer. "Just got it. I can do all sorts on it – broadband Internet, MP3 downloads – Aidan would go nuts for it – but it's really to help me watch the weather."

"Not all your swag is going into a trust, then."

"An insurance company bought it for me."

"Why?"

"I tip them off about storms, save a few lives, and they give me a computer – and send a token of their appreciation."

Erika smiled. "It's all right for a weather prophet."

Jake was suddenly alert. Reflecting his change of mood, behind Erika, TC let out a low growl. "Why call me that?"

"Because that's what you are."

Jake had come across the term only in his father's letter. Had she seen it? "You could have said a weather forecaster or whatever. Why a weather prophet?"

"Well, excuse me," Erika replied indignantly. "I'll be more careful with my words in future. I don't know. It just sounds good. Like, forecasters get it wrong, prophets get it right."

Jake stared at her yet saw only innocence. "All right. Sorry. It's just that . . . Never mind." Instead, he turned to the monitor and said, "See? That's the coast of Senegal, Africa. It's like looking down from space. You've got one, two, three, four splodges of cloud over the sea. They're thunderstorms. A satellite's taking pictures of them and a weather plane's tracking them. Over the last hour or two, they've got a bit closer together."

Looking at the screen over his shoulder, she said, "So what?"

He ignored the smell of her perfume wafting over him. "Early days, but you'll be hearing about them on the news if – when – they join forces. They'll make a tropical storm then a hurricane."

"Fascinating," Erika muttered sarcastically as she dropped onto his bed. "How's work?"

He turned towards her. "Good."

"Mum said you'd made a big impression. Like, you even got the boss out of his office."

Jake nodded. "I showed them how you could move a storm to stop one lot of people getting hurt – and how you heap the misery on another lot of people. That pretty much sums it up."

"You can really do that?"

"No." Jake looked into Erika's face and, keeping his voice down, he asked, "What exactly does your mum do at Castleton?"

"Exactly? I don't know. Never asked. I'm not really interested. It's just Mum."

Jake sighed. It struck him that a girl he really fancied was sitting on his bed, chatting to him, and all he'd done was talk about the weather and Castleton Computing. But, as soon as he stopped talking about the weather, he dried up.

The doorbell chimed again and Tin Can barked. The robot turned to tackle the stairs once more. He'd barely started the laborious task when Jake's mum shouted, "Busy night. It's Aidan. On his way up."

"Wotcher, boy," Aidan said as he stepped over TC. "Superstar DJ in the house. No need to bite." Entering Jake's bedroom, he came to an abrupt halt. "Oh, sorry. I didn't know you two were . . ."

Erika completed his sentence for him. "Talking about the weather."

"Is that what you call it?" Aidan replied with a smirk.

"No. *Really* talking about the weather."

"I know." Mischievously, Aidan added, "That's all Jake does. Pure as the driven snow, he is." Then his eyes shifted enviously to the new computer. "Wow!"

Jake smiled. "That's what Erika said as well."

Aidan plonked himself down in front of the monitor without invitation. "I'll have to load some software on it for you so I can mix music round here."

"And that's for me, is it?" Jake asked.

"Well . . ."

"Doesn't sound like I get much out of it."

"You do," Aidan replied.

"What's that, then?"

Aidan turned back towards Jake. "You said Castleton Computing might've nicked . . ." He glanced at Erika and added, "You know. Anyway, I talked to Mum for you. I hope you appreciate the sacrifice – a mark of true friendship. I wouldn't have talked to her for anyone else. In a week or two – whenever she can – she'll email you a file of everything her paper's got on Castleton." He looked at Erika again and said, "Don't tell your mum."

Erika shrugged. "No idea what you're talking about, and I'm not interested. So, nothing to tell and no reason to."

Aidan nodded. "Good, because Mum said it's pretty spicy. Some of it's so spicy, their solicitor wouldn't let them publish it."

CHAPTER 17

On Saturday afternoon, Carly almost spilled her wine. She looked at the slim piece of paper again, choked and coughed. "You got this in this morning's post?"

Jake nodded.

"You haven't been putting all your money on a horse, have you?"

"Yes. I backed a long shot called Tennessee Tornado."

Carly smiled. "It must've had a fair wind behind it. A thousand pounds is a hell of a win."

"It's a token of Henson's appreciation," Jake replied, unable to stop a grin spreading right across his face.

"They're a very appreciative company." She hesitated and then added, "It's another contribution to your trust, you know. I don't want this sort of money sitting in your building society account. You'd only splash it all on sex, drugs, and rock and roll."

Jake looked severely at his mum. "I wouldn't!"

Carly squeezed his shoulder. "Only kidding. I know you wouldn't. You'd spend it on weather stuff – but now you've got all you could possibly want. So . . ."

"A new digital camera would be good. Really high resolution."

"All right," Carly conceded.

"And a new mobile."

Carly put up a hand. "Stop! We get you a new mobile and a camera, and the rest goes into savings."

The input for the supercomputer came from satellites, national weather services all around the globe, ships, observers in commercial aircraft and military bases, automatic weather stations and floating buoys, and Castleton's unmanned aerial vehicles. The UAVs flew under Carly Patmore's programming to take measurements from out-of-the-way places, like parts of the Pacific Ocean.

At work after school on Monday, Jake clicked on the icon for Castleton Computing's first weather satellite, CC1, and at once he got a splash of information on its current status. It was taking pictures of clouds with visible light and infrared radiation, providing radar images of rainfall, and recording wind speed and direction, water vapour, and variations in temperature with altitude. The second satellite was keeping its eye on the conditions off the coast of Africa. Over the weekend, the four storms had combined into one tropical depression and CC2 was monitoring it.

When Jake double-clicked on the icons for weather satellites CC3 and CC4, the system denied him access to any information on their operation. At once, his mind turned to his dad's letter. *Recently, the model has locked me out of some parts of its programming. Some high-up in Castleton will be behind that.* With an unpleasant tingle running down his back, Jake wondered if Castleton's newest satellites did more than simply observe the atmosphere. Perhaps they did something the company didn't want him to know about.

Brian slipped into the room and said, "You're looking at a potential hurricane there. If the depression intensifies over the next forty-eight hours, it'll be a beauty. But if the upper winds increase, they'll pull it apart before it comes of age."

Jake shook his head. "It's going to be a monster."

Brian laughed. "One thing I've learned already – not to bet against you. Anyway, come on. Work time. You've got to repeat the meteorological equivalent of moving mountains."

The big blot romping across the Atlantic was turning into a phenomenal weather system. By Tuesday, it had been declared a tropical storm. The rotation of the planet set it spinning. Then, breathing the moist sun-warmed air lying on the ocean, it puffed itself up until it was six miles high. On Wednesday, it joined the big boys.

With excitement in his voice, Brian said, "Have you heard? It's been upgraded. The National Hurricane

Center has named it. You're watching Hurricane Alberto."

On the monitor, images of the newly-formed hurricane were electronically enhanced and colour-coded. On the left-hand side of the split screen, the zones of heaviest rainfall were marked in orange and yellow. Around the dead eye of the storm, the vivid colour spiralled impressively. Further out from the black hole at its centre, there was a large area of blue and green where the rainfall was merely lashing rather than torrential. The display on the right was graded for temperature. This time, the empty hole at the hurricane's centre was white. A ragged red ring indicating the highest coldest cloud looked like blood diffusing out of the eye. The bright stain ran into a blue oval that gave way to a yellow that abandoned all notion of symmetry. In these outlying areas, where the hurricane lost its well-defined shape, the cloud was warmer and more scattered. Senegal was a featureless black bulge on the right.

"US Hurricane Hunters are parachuting instrument packages into it," Brian announced. "Look at the barometer reading. Have you seen what the supercomputer's predicting now? It's saying the pressure'll go down to 865 millibars in five or six days. That'd be a record. This," he said, pointing at his screen, "is a storm on steroids."

Jake nodded. Over the years, he'd kept weather

records. He knew that the lowest ever atmospheric pressure at sea level was 870 millibars, recorded in 1979 at the eye of Typhoon Tip. And that typhoon produced fierce winds across a width of 1,100 km.

The experts were fretting more and more as Alberto lumbered towards the coast of the USA, getting meaner and meaner as he went. Timo Scarpa had emailed Jake twice about the hurricane. Yet it was too soon to predict its exact course. It wasn't going to be good news for America, though. National meteorological offices, Castleton's weather model and Jake were monitoring Alberto's every twist and turn. Lots of computers were churning away, calculating its likely path. The first results would be little better than guesses. As the hurricane approached the Caribbean, the guesses would be updated and refined. They'd become firm estimates, then precise predictions.

Once Alberto's destiny had been fixed, islands that found themselves in his way could batten down the hatches and the threatened part of mainland America could prepare for the worst.

Down the road in Sheffield, a more modest thunderstorm drifted, rumbled and crackled overhead. To Jake, though, it was just as remarkable as Hurricane Alberto. It was extraordinary because he hadn't seen it coming. It was as if he'd stood beside a road, checked that it was clear both ways, stepped out, and been crushed by a thundering lorry. He felt flustered and suddenly fallible. Perhaps Alberto, unexpected cheques and moving meteorological mountains had distracted him so he hadn't got wind of the weather in his own backyard.

He stood near the doorway of his house, watching. It was a strange storm, highly localised. The evening had not yet given way to night so Jake could see the curtain of rain to the east – less than a mile away, he guessed. The concentrated squall was dripping with electricity, so Jake readied his camera, expecting lightning at any second. He didn't have to wait for long. In the cumulonimbus, crystals of ice jostled against each other, like rubbing a balloon against wool, to produce an electrical charge. The negative charges at the base of the cloud carved a crooked, invisible route to positive charges on the ground. The return stroke – positive charges shooting upwards to the cloud along the same channels – made the visible flash.

Jake muttered a curse as he took the photograph a split-second too late to capture the glowing streaks of air. Still, it wasn't dark enough for a really spectacular photo.

For less than a second, the air in the lightning's path became hotter than the surface of the sun. The sudden expansion caused a sharp explosion and its shock wave radiated outwards. The thunder hit Jake three seconds later, meaning that lightning had struck a kilometre away. He peered to his left and wondered where it had vented its anger.

Luckily, the local press office was deserted on Friday evening when lightning ripped through it. No one was hurt. But the power surge wiped out the newspaper's central processor and the fire that followed destroyed the backup CD-ROM version of its archives. By the time that the storm petered out, Mrs Webb's collection of spicy information on Castleton Computing no longer existed.

Jake knew that there were about 300,000 ground strikes in Britain every year. Perhaps it wasn't so unlikely that the local press office would be hit. Even so, it was quite a coincidence . . . Perhaps there was another explanation. Perhaps he wasn't fallible after all. Perhaps Brian Mosby was a modern-day medicine man using the supercomputer as his totem pole for conjuring up a lightning bolt on an enemy target.

CHAPTER 18

It was morning break on Tuesday the 4th of July and Cosmic Cosgrove was pointing to the Internet news on his computer monitor. *Hurricane Alberto Claims Low-pressure Record*. "This is going to spoil all those American parties. They'll be getting in a panic with a category-five hurricane headed in their direction." He shook his head. "It'll be blamed on global warming, of course. That's the trendy scapegoat for any nasty weather. Still, I'm glad I'm not in the Caribbean or anywhere near. That is where it's going, isn't it?"

"Just about," Jake replied.

"Has Castleton's system projected landfall yet?"

Jake shook his head. "Somewhere between Cuba and South Carolina. It'll narrow it down, but not yet. I'll pinpoint it tomorrow." He paused before adding, "If I haven't lost my knack. I didn't see Friday's storm till it was on top of us."

Cosmic took hold of a pile of exercise books. "Neither did anyone else. So, like the rest of us, you're human. Keep it in proportion, Jake. That's one you got wrong, out of how many hundreds?"

"Do you know if anyone's ever made the weather?"

Sensing a serious conversation, Cosmic put down the books. "*Made* it?"

"Yeah. Like a thunderstorm."

"Creating rain's been on people's agendas for years. Egyptians performed rainmaking rituals around 3,500 BC. Imagine yourself living in a desert or near a raging forest fire. You'd pray for rain – or maybe try to seed it. A couple of weeks back, I read an article about something called carbon black," Cosmic said. "It's a dust that soaks up solar energy. When it's scattered in the air over the nearest bit of water, the dust gets hot. That heats the air and makes the water evaporate more. That's the theory as far as I recall. The warm air rises and, when it gets cold higher up – especially if it's in the cool of the evening – the water vapour condenses out. That means a rainstorm. Maybe even a thunderstorm."

"So," Jake replied, "I might not have been wrong about Friday's weather because someone might've made it."

Cosmic looked puzzled. "That's a bit far-fetched, just to preserve your one-hundred-per-cent record! You could admit you made one wee error."

Jake wasn't going to admit anything.

"Why would anyone want to do that?" Cosmic continued. "Sheffield isn't exactly suffering a drought. No forest fires."

Jake didn't answer aloud, but he could think of one very good reason why someone would want to blast the press office with lightning. In particular, he knew why someone would want to destroy the electronic file on Castleton Computing. But who, other than Mrs Webb, knew she was going to email it to him? Aidan and Erika Ray. That's all. So, who was the traitor? Who told the storm-making medicine man at Castleton? Not Aidan. Besides, it didn't make sense to accuse Aidan or his mum. If they hadn't wanted Jake to get his hands on the information, they wouldn't have offered to send it to him in the first place. That left only one suspect – the girl he fancied. The girl who had an easy link to Castleton Computing via her mother. The girl who'd called him a weather prophet, perhaps letting slip that she'd seen his dad's stolen letter. The girl who'd started mixing with him again for no obvious reason.

Cosmic probably wanted to change the subject but he almost seemed to read Jake's mind. "I've seen you hanging out with Erika Ray recently."

"Yes."

The Geordie Geography teacher could turn on his natural dialect at will. "Aye, she's a bonny lass. Good on yer."

Jake reddened.

Cosmic grinned at him. "You're not so different from the other boys after all – obsessing about girls, sex, spots and being cool. Makes a change from the weather. By the way," he added, "the school's had a request from Castleton."

"What sort of request?"

"They want you on work experience," Cosmic answered. "The head's delegated it to me."

Jake's heart rate leaped. He needed more time at the company if he was going to get to the bottom of everything. "What do you think?"

Cosmic smiled. "The timing's pretty good. Year 10. I think we can spare you for the last two weeks of term. You'll be a full-time worker from Monday. All right?"

"Thanks, sir," Jake replied. He was about to gush, but he paused, holding himself in check.

"What is it?"

Hesitantly, Jake said, "Well, would you work for a company that made things into weapons?"

Cosmic let out a long breath. "That's a tricky one. We need some weapons – for defence – but I'd draw the line somewhere. Myself, I'd never work on nuclear, chemical or biological weapons. But, hey, what do I know? I'm just an asylum seeker from Geordie land." He hesitated and then said, "Of course, we're all asylum seekers. I seek asylum from school at footie matches. Aidan does it with music. You? If you think someone's turning the weather into a weapon, you'll need asylum. Erika maybe."

Jake shook his head.

"Your mum?"

"She works at Castleton."

Cosmic nodded. "OK, but I think you can trust your own mum, Jake. Anyway, you can always have a chat with me, if you like."

Jake looked down at the floor. "Do you have a dad, sir?"

"I do. Yes. He's a headteacher. Must be in the Cosgrove genes. He's proud of me." Cosmic waited until Jake looked at him and then he added, "Your dad would be proud of you too. And I bet he'd trust you to work out your own morality – not his or mine. Your own. But I will say this. You don't want to play David to Castleton's Goliath. No contest."

The buzzer sounded the end of break.

Cosmic groaned. "No rest for the wicked, is there? Where are you due next?"

Jake pulled a face. "English."

"What are you tackling?"

"Shakespeare. *The Tempest*."

Cosmic smiled wryly. "Mmm. Very apt."

Jake sauntered towards the classroom door and, holding it open, halted. Turning back, he said, "David beat Goliath, didn't he?"

"It's a myth, Jake."

The next evening, an anxious Timo Scarpa was on the phone straight after Jake got home from Castleton.

"Where's it going to land, Jake? Are the forecasts right?"

Jake knew immediately what the insurer had on his mind. "Yes. A hurricane's the best-understood weather system. Everyone's saying the same thing. Me too. It's going to shoot between Cuba and the Bahamas and run slap bang into Miami."

"But you're talking two hundred mile-an-hour winds in the eye wall – and ten-metre waves."

"Yes."

"They're considering evacuating the place right now. The celebrities are already leaving their islands in the bay. You don't want to know how much Tom Cruise has got himself and his property insured for. Anyway, that sort of force will collapse the bridges and smash a lot of luxury homes and hotels. And there are always a few ocean liners in the bay. If even one of them comes to grief . . . Well, the payout's astronomical. If Alberto makes a direct hit on Miami, it won't be far short of a hundred billion dollars in damage. That'll sink the whole insurance business."

"What can I say?"

"Just tell me the eye wall will miss Miami," Timo said desperately.

"I can't do that."

"Shares are in freefall right now. Everyone's bracing themselves for a stock-market crash. They think the insurance industry's going down."

Jake said, "I'll let you know if there's any change."

"Yeah. Thanks. And pray for divine intervention."

Brian Mosby appeared relaxed. The chic meteorologist had none of Timo Scarpa's stress. "You'll remember a couple of summers back. August and September 2004 were rough for Florida and the Caribbean, to say the least. First, Hurricane Charley arrived on Friday the thirteenth, killing twenty-seven people in Florida. Three weeks later, it was Hurricane Frances and another twenty-odd lives. Between them, they did something like nine billion pounds' worth of damage. Then the big one rolled in. Hurricane Ivan – Ivan the Terrible, the press called it. The wind ripped half Grenada's homes up and threw them away. It took the roofs off ninety per cent of the buildings. Torrential rain and eight-metre waves didn't help, either. Sixty people dead in Grenada and Jamaica, and a hundred altogether. Trees collapsed on houses, the electricity supply went down, and road bridges got swept away.

"To finish the region off, tropical storm Jeanne flooded the Dominican Republic and Haiti, drowning hundreds of people. That's what I call a wet and windy couple of months. Just think of the lives, money and property we could save if we could do something about it." Brian was making it clear that he could justify tampering with the weather and that he believed it was right to do so. Without giving Jake an opportunity to respond, he tapped the screen of his monitor. "Now Alberto comes along at exactly the right time. It gives you a live storm to play with. No simulation this time. If you wanted to save the good citizens of Miami from total devastation, how would you do it?"

Jake gulped at the thought. "It's a three-hundred-mile-wide hurricane!"

"That's why it's a good candidate. Everyone in the area's going to get roughed up, but the eye wall – the worst of it – will definitely be over Miami. So, how would you shift Alberto somewhere less important?"

The supercomputer gave Jake a black-and-white view of the top of Alberto, superimposed on a map. Running at many times faster than natural speed, the deepest depression on Earth rushed down its predicted path to the heart of Miami and slammed full tilt into the coastal city.

Before Jake had decided where he'd try his first intervention, the door opened and, unusually, Gordon Dell entered. At once, the boss said, "Don't mind me. And don't let me put you off. Carry on."

Jake concentrated on his screen again while Brian and Gordon focused on the other networked computer. There was no doubt in Jake's mind that they were monitoring his efforts.

"This is difficult," Jake told them. "If I – we – steer it north, we wipe out the Bahamas. If we kept it south of the Bahamas but north of Miami, it'll hit Fort

Lauderdale and West Palm Beach. I don't know what's there but . . ."

Gordon peered over the top of the monitors with a smirk. "I do. I've been there. Lots of expensive water-front homes. Very plush. Rich people with their own boats. Some would say they deserve a hurricane. Anyway, that'd be better than letting Miami bear the brunt."

Jake ignored his crass comment. "If we try to move it south, it hits Cuba or it goes into the Gulf of Mexico. Then it could crash into somewhere like Galveston." Jake remembered from his notes that the town had been tortured once before – in the days before hurricanes were personalised with names. *8th September 1900. Hurricane destroyed half of Galveston, Texas, and the storm surge took 8,000 lives, about a third of the city's population.*

Brian said, "Politically, Cuba's less important."

Jake hoped that Brian was joking. "Isn't it people who are important?"

"Quite right," Gordon replied.

"Anyway, it's all fantasy, isn't it? We can't really move a hurricane."

Gordon's eyes glanced upwards. "Someone up there might be able to do it. The Americans will be praying. They're better at it than us."

Jake's interventions were more sci-fi than divine. By heating the air on one side of Alberto's path or the

144

other, Jake changed its anticipated course slightly – but not enough. He made the eye strike the Everglades National Park, south of Miami; or Miami Beach and Hollywood to the north, but part of the eye wall always cut through the city.

He instructed the computer to show him the current position of Alberto and asked for a mass of very warm air to form immediately behind it and to the south. He hoped that, because the storm would be attracted to the warmth, his make-believe intervention would act as a brake, and drag Alberto south.

Running the sequence, the computer calculated that the hurricane's eye would skirt around the Everglades and skim across the edge of Cuba. It would pummel the Florida Keys, fly into the Gulf of Mexico and curve north, making landfall fairly harmlessly in Louisiana between Galveston and New Orleans.

Two gleeful heads appeared either side of the monitor opposite. Simultaneously, Brian and Gordon cried, "Perfect."

Brian said, "Right. Run it again, Jake. Let's see if you can hit it straight down the fairway no matter how close the storm is to Miami when you change it."

"OK."

It mattered a lot, Jake found. "*If* you could heat the sea," he concluded, "you'd have to do it in the next three hours. After that, the hurricane wouldn't turn in time and Miami would still cop it."

To Jake's surprise, Gordon and Brian stared at each other for a moment and then Gordon got up. He strode out of the computer room, saying, "Don't do anything until I say so."

Jake looked into Brian's face. "What's going on? You can't really . . . Can you?"

Brian gazed back at Jake. "I'm not at liberty . . . You'll have to ask Gordon or Neisha. But I think your job's done for the day. Brilliant. You can go home and get some well-earned rest – or crack on with homework."

CHAPTER 19

Colonel Emery B Husband Jr. of the US Air Force, Weapons Procurement Division, was sitting bolt upright as always. "Mr Dell. What can I do for you, sir?"

"It's more a matter of what my company can do for you."

"You have something to report since our last conversation?"

"I don't want to waste your time talking about the value of our technology to the military. We've already agreed in principle the benefits of manipulating the weather. Now, I want to give you a practical demonstration."

"Go on," the colonel urged. "You're on a secure line."

"You said you saw environmental modification as an important strategic weapon of the future. In the next few hours, I can convince you it's an important strategic weapon of the present."

"Are you referring to Hurricane Alberto by any chance?"

Gordon checked his watch. "In twenty-eight hours, it will ravage Miami. Yes?"

147

Emery agreed. "Our troops are assisting evacuation right now. It's bigger than Hurricane Ivan two years ago, apparently, and we stockpiled ten thousand body bags for that one. We didn't need them in the end because it missed the big cities. This time, I've got twenty thousand body bags ready."

"A sensible – and chilling – precaution," Gordon replied. "You've got a weapon equivalent to a multi-megaton nuclear bomb coming in your direction." He paused for effect. "But I can deflect it – if I give the order in the next couple of hours or so."

"I'm listening, Mr Dell."

"I can't go into methodology. Not until you've seen the demonstration and expressed an economic interest. It won't weaken the hurricane but it will steer it onto a new course—"

The Head of the USAF Weapons Procurement Division interrupted. "I'd be failing in my duty if I didn't ask where you'd move the hurricane to. As a military man, any control over its path is significant but, as an American citizen, I want to know that what you're proposing is safe."

"Quite right, Colonel. I could have gone ahead without contacting you because my company's intervention will be invisible. But, to convince you, I had to call you beforehand. If I'd told you afterwards, it would have been hard to persuade you that an unexpected turn of events was an act of Castleton Computing rather than an act of God. In a matter of hours, your National Hurricane Center will note that Alberto is veering from its predicted path. You'll need to evacuate Florida Keys and your oil rigs in the Gulf. Key West will take a direct hit. The wind and rain in Miami will be ferocious – they'll still need to fasten their seatbelts – but we'll push the eye wall into the Gulf of Mexico, grazing Cuba. It'll go ashore in the US, I'm afraid. There's no escaping that."

"There's no chance of it running into New Orleans, is there? It's below sea level, you know. That would be the worst possible scenario. We'd have all our resources shutting down Miami and the Keys while a hurricane brings New Orleans to its knees."

"No. It'll be up to your meteorologists to track it but, I'll tell you now, it'll hit a sparsely populated area of Louisiana. I'll email the grid reference where our model says it will go."

"Very well."

Gordon's voiced dripped with self-satisfaction. "I'd advise you to tune your TV to a weather station. It won't be long. I'll expect to hear from you after that."

Jake Patmore, the media, Timo Scarpa, the whole insurance industry, and hundreds of weather forecasters stared at the latest predictions, hardly daring to believe what was happening. Hurricane Alberto was drifting south of its anticipated course. Miami and the

Everglade swamps would be mauled by furious wind and rain but the belly of the storm would pass between Cuba and Florida. Alberto had sprung a surprise. For Colonel Emery B Husband Jr., Gordon Dell and Brian Mosby, though, the hurricane's manoeuvre was not a shock. For them, it was a huge relief.

Jake had plenty of bad-weather friends – people who wanted to know him when severe weather threatened – but he didn't believe they were fair-weather friends as well. He watched Alberto on his home computer, feeling exploited. He was certain that the staff at Castleton had deceived him. He could not accept that there had been two divine interventions in a matter of days. First, an unforeseen thunderbolt had hit the newspaper office that was about to send him an incriminating document about Castleton Computing. Now, Hurricane Alberto hiccupped and, out of the blue, took off down a path that should have been a figment of the weather model's imagination. What's more, the isotherms behind and to the south of the storm indicated that the air had warmed inexplicably.

Jake didn't object to Castleton saving people's lives and property by persuading a hurricane to avoid a city, but he had his doubts. Three doubts. He wondered what the knock-on effects would be. If the flap of a butterfly's wing on one side of the globe could rain off a barbeque on the other side, interfering with hurricanes or making local thunderstorms could lead to dramatic distant changes. The end of one nation's drought is another nation's catastrophic flooding.

Jake couldn't believe that Castleton's motives were purely benevolent. If preventing misery were their only aim, right now they'd be shouting from the rooftops about their success with Alberto. Their secrecy suggested something much more sinister to Jake. And that was Jake's third doubt. Why was the company not being open and honest with him?

If he needed to talk things through, who *were* his all-weather friends? Aidan, Grandad Patmore and Mr Cosgrove. Possibly Robert Goodhart at the university as well. And TC, of course. Cosmic was probably right: he should include his mum. But he didn't. If he told her that Castleton had somehow learned how to fiddle with the weather, she would almost certainly accuse him of living in dreamland. If he told her that he thought the company might be doing it to impress the armed forces, no doubt she'd accuse him of being as neurotic as his father.

He needed proof of Castleton's intentions. His instinct was telling him to step up his espionage. His dad had told him always to follow his instinct.

Four and a half thousand miles away from Sheffield, a colossal wave capsized two pleasure cruisers. It also picked up two yachts in the marina and dumped them both in the deserted car park of a hotel. Miami's palm trees were bent double by Alberto's vicious wind. After its passing, the palms left standing looked like giant matchsticks stuck in the ground. There was merely a bulge at the upper end because the storm had plucked out every single frond. The streets were littered with fallen road signs, great pools of seawater, foliage, and hoardings. A few vehicles had been turned over and lay on their sides or backs like dead insects. The people were without an electricity supply, yet they were lucky. They had avoided the centre of the storm that would have brought winds twice as fast, a few cruel minutes of calm and then a second hammering as the opposite wall of the eye rolled inland. Best of all, they had avoided the storm surge that would have swept swollen seawater through the streets.

For the duration of the passing storm, the tranquil water of the Everglade swamps became choppy and foamed like breaking sea. While Alberto rampaged through the National Park, its alligators took refuge in deep holes and large-leafed lilies were ripped from their roots. Several airboats were whisked away from their moorings and never seen again.

Barrelling relentlessly past Cuba, Alberto ransacked tourist beaches, destroyed its tobacco industry, and sliced through shantytowns like a circular saw. The wind dismantled people's homes bit by bit. First, it got under the eaves and lifted the roofs. The corrugated sheets stood up like sails, detached themselves from the shacks, and took off. Then each of the four flimsy walls collapsed in turn until there was nothing. Trees were stripped bare of foliage and uprooted. Anything left upright was dashed by storm surges and half-buried by sliding mud. When the storm had finished with the island, it looked as if massive bombs had exploded all along Cuba's coastline.

Once Hurricane Alberto had crashed into Louisiana, it was denied its source of energy by the land, and it began to wither like a tired athlete. Within hours, it was downgraded to a tropical storm. Even so, for twenty-four hours, it drenched everything in six southeastern states and its high winds caused havoc. It spawned several tornadoes in Arkansas and closed all major East Coast airports. By the time that Alberto died in Missouri, it was responsible for hundreds of injuries and nineteen deaths, eighteen of them on Cuba. Fifteen people were drowned in high surf or mud, two were killed by objects that Alberto made into missiles, one woman suffered a heart attack, and another was electrocuted by a falling power line in Lafayette, Louisiana.

To Gordon Dell, the whole episode was a great advert for Castleton's abilities and for brute force. To Miami and the insurance industry, it was a reprieve. To the uninsured of Cuba, it was a disaster that took away their homes, their families and their livelihoods. To Jake, it confirmed that he was part of a game that churned his stomach. It confirmed everything that his dad had written.

Downstairs, his mum was watching an old film on TV with the usual glass of white wine in her hand. Jake sat down opposite her and took a deep breath. "How come we don't talk about Dad?" he asked.

At once, the film was forgotten. "What?"

"Don't you miss him?"

Carly's normally unshakeable bubbly exterior dried up and she collapsed into misery. It was an amazing transition, like watching dark clouds obliterate a clear sky. His mum's sudden squall came from trauma, long suppressed. "We got a lousy rotten deal, your dad and me. We signed up for a lifetime and we got eight years. Eight years! We were cheated."

"Sorry, Mum. I didn't mean—"

Interrupting him, Carly pointed at the television. "You know why I'm watching this? I saw it with your dad. It was our first trip to the cinema together." She shook her head miserably. "When your dad died, everything went black for me. You – and work – were my only lights. Nine years later, I cope by working and not thinking about it. If I do think about it, I keep it to myself. As for talking . . . all the talking in the world won't bring him back." She dabbed at her eyes. "I'm not like Grandad Patmore, Jake. I moved on. I didn't have a choice. I had a kid to clothe and feed."

"But you've got memories of him. I can hardly

remember anything. Just him sitting at the computer and doing things with the weather station in the garden."

A shattered smile came to Carly's face. "I know. I'm sorry. Obviously you didn't take it in, but I spent hours talking to you about him at bedtime. Other kids got fairy stories with happy endings; you got my thoughts about your dad. Your face. You couldn't understand why he'd gone."

"Tell me about him again," said Jake.

Carly poured herself another large drink and shook her head. "Let go. He's long gone. Do you think he'd want me to harp on about it?"

Jake shrugged. He didn't reply because he suspected that the answer was no.

"Fifteen-year-old boys don't hug their mums, do they?" Carly muttered. "It's a no-go area."

Jake mumbled, "That's right," and went back upstairs.

CHAPTER 20

Tin Can looked at Erika warily yet expectantly. If he'd been a real dog, he would have been on his guard but still hopeful that she would offer him a chocolatey treat. His reaction reflected the ebb and flow of Jake's feelings for her.

"You heard about Hurricane Alberto?" Jake asked her.

"No," Erika replied. "It didn't affect me."

Jake had decided what to do about his charming traitor. He needed to feed her some false information and then wait to see if and where it emerged. He said, "I'm thinking of quitting Castleton."

"You're joking! Why?"

"Because they're not being honest with me."

"What planet are you on?" Erika exclaimed. "An honest business? No chance. Adults don't work to those sorts of rules."

Jake shrugged sadly.

"And what about all that cash you're raking in?"

He leaped at the chance to plant a lie. "Don't tell your mum but I'm still working for three insurance companies. They pay me bucketfuls." Jake had just grumbled about Castleton's dishonesty, but his was different. His was justified.

"Well, it's up to you, I suppose. I just think it's daft to throw away your celebrity status at Castleton. You're made for life there."

"Why have you come round, Erika?"

Taken aback by his blunt question, Erika's mouth opened but, for a moment, no words emerged. At the second attempt, she said, "Because you're a celebrity. Because, despite everything, you're . . . cute."

"Like Chewy the rat."

"No. You're screwy, serious and nerdy as well as cute." She hesitated before adding with a grin, "And getting richer by the minute."

For someone shifty, Erika seemed sincere. Jake was disarmed by her frank reply.

Changing the subject quickly, she said, "I've got a plan. We go to school – yes, I know it's Sunday – for Aidan's gig. Well, someone's got to, and we're his mates. Then the three of us check out a movie at the Showroom."

"When you leave school, you'll be in the police or a teacher or something. Somewhere you can boss everybody about."

She laughed. "You might be right. But what do you say? Deal?"

"What's the film?"

"Thought you'd never ask. *The Storm Chaser*. Get your coat on."

How could he resist?

Aidan appreciated the surround-sound effects that seemed to make their seats vibrate. Erika ogled the male lead, and Jake saw the storms coming before anyone else in the cinema. He didn't need the cue of sinister low-pitched music.

In a scene where nothing of interest was happening – just some cheesy romance brewing – Jake looked sideways at Erika and wondered. He wished he could be wrong about her. He wished she wasn't seeing him merely to pass information to her mother. Jake also wondered about his own mum, sitting in a cinema all those years ago on a date with Dad. Had his dad looked sideways at her and wondered what would happen between them? He must have gazed into her face and trusted her completely.

When Erika turned and glanced at him with a smile, Jake's heartbeat accelerated. In the semi-darkness, he could have mistaken her for a would-be girlfriend. But she was just an actress.

In front of them, the close-up kissing continued. It was the calm before the storm.

Gordon Dell was sitting coolly behind his desk. He lifted his left leg up onto his right and wrapped both hands around the shin. Neisha Ray was leaning against the wall on the right, next to the window. Beyond her, altostratus formed a grey sheet like frosted glass in front of the morning sun. It was Monday, the first day of Jake's full-time job at the company. Jake was seated next to his mother, opposite the head of Castleton Computing.

"I don't know what all the fuss is about," Gordon was saying. "Miami suffered a near-miss rather than a bull's-eye. As a result, a lot of people and properties are still standing."

Jake didn't dare look into Gordon's face as he replied, "You said, 'Don't do anything till I say so,' and left the room. Next thing, Hurricane Alberto did exactly what I'd worked out with the weather model. That can't be a coincidence."

"Quite right," Gordon replied with a warm smile, as if he were about to explain something simple to an errant child. "We're merely carrying on your dad's good work – and taking it to the next stage, just as he'd want." He glanced at Carly and then back at Jake. "We knew there'd come a time when it'd be obvious we've developed certain technology since your father . . . worked here. Alberto was the crunch moment. We couldn't hide the fact that we've learned to influence a storm, so . . . here we are. With an excellent result. Now, you've been with us for long enough, Jake, so I can trust you with what I'm about to say." Again, he looked at Carly. "I recognise that the whole Patmore family has been – and remains – a faithful friend to Castleton Computing. And I think Castleton is very important to the Patmore household."

Jake thought that Dell had the knack of making even an ordinary sentence sound threatening.

Carly nodded faintly, waiting.

Gordon continued, "You know yourself, Jake, that predicting the weather can be very profitable from an insurance point of view. Modifying it would be even more cost-effective and, of course, lessen people's misery enormously."

So, Dell knew about Jake's relationship with Henson Insurance. But it wasn't such a big secret. His mum had probably talked to Neisha about it. Either of them might have mentioned it to Gordon Dell.

Gordon chuckled. "I don't mind you fleecing Henson's at all – good for you – but I wonder if they'll carry on."

"What do you mean?" asked Jake.

"Well, they'll look at Alberto and think you – like everyone else – got it wrong. They might not believe your predictions from now on."

It seemed to Jake that Gordon was challenging him to respond. "I could tell them you altered it."

Gordon seemed pleased with Jake's remark. He nodded. "Feel free. Tell all the insurance companies you're in contact with."

160

That was it. The moment that Jake had been antici-pating and dreading. It was plain that Gordon Dell had received the false information that he was helping three insurance companies and not just Henson's. It was proof that Erika Ray was the snake in the grass. He avoided looking at Neisha with an accusing stare.

Gordon's comment told Jake two more things. He gathered that the Weather-Modification Team regarded the insurance sector as a customer for its expertise. It was also clear that the company was exploiting him again. This time, he was expected to attract the atten-tion of Timo Scarpa and others in the same line of business.

"Let me get this straight, Gordon," Carly said. "With Jake's help, you can modify the weather . . ."

"Imagine staging a marathon where no one could agree on a starting place and time. It'd be chaos. Jake gives us a sensible start. Craig's computer does the rest."

"And you want to sell this . . . commodity to insurers and the like?" she asked.

"Yes."

"Is that the only reason: saving everyone's misery?"

Gordon nodded. "As I recall, that was a big motiva-tional factor for Craig. You'll know better than me. Anyway, we're getting close to making his dream come true."

"How?"

Gordon uncrossed his legs and looked more formal for the first time. "Now that's something I do have to keep under wraps for a while. You'll understand there are patents to sort out, competitors to put off."

Jake cut in, saying, "I know you can heat a fair chunk of air – and maybe water as well." He also knew that Alberto had come suspiciously early in the season for a major hurricane. "Did you create the storms off Senegal in the first place?"

"Making tropical storms from scratch would be a considerable achievement."

"And dangerous."

"Quite right."

Jake persisted. "But did you?"

"No."

There were a few seconds of silence before Carly asked Jake, "Are we satisfied with that, then? Has that cleared it up?"

"I suppose so," Jake said in a hushed voice.

Gordon slapped his desk with his palm. "Excellent. We can all get back to work."

Of course Jake wasn't satisfied, but he'd had enough of this confrontation. Besides, he knew Gordon would sidestep the real questions about weather warfare.

CHAPTER 21

At lunchtime the next day, Jake slipped out of work to
visit Dr Robert Goodhart in the university's
Department of Natural Sciences. When Jake walked
cagily into Robert's office, the academic looked surprised but pleased to see him.

"How are you doing, Jake?"

He felt like a fish out of water. He was a school kid
moving in an unfamiliar adult world, not helpless but
certainly not in control. He looked around the room.
Filing cabinets, desk, computer, charts and maps and
timetables on the wall. "Well . . ."

"Sit down. How are you getting on at Castleton?"

"In a way, good." He was wondering how to voice
his unease when Robert interrupted.

"But you're bothered. Otherwise you wouldn't be
here. What can I do for you?"

"I just wondered if you . . ."

"What?" asked Robert, with a friendly smile.

"Do you know Castleton?"

"Pretty well. They've funded some of my research in

163

the past. My main contacts were Brian Mosby and Gordon Dell. Brian was a student here as well."

Jake asked, "What do you think of him?"

"He's very enthusiastic and thorough, but not particularly inspirational. He's a very efficient workhorse, but nowhere near as imaginative as you."

"He's in charge of altering the weather."

Dr Goodhart frowned. "I know he's in charge of their Weather-Modification Team, but that's all theory and research. Isn't it?"

"No."

"What?"

"When Hurricane Alberto changed its mind about where to go, that was Castleton."

"You're joking!"

Jake shook his head.

"Are you sure?" Robert said. "It's not your creative side gone into overdrive, is it?"

"No. I was the one who worked out how you could stop it hitting Miami – just before it did exactly what I said."

Trust in Jake was displacing the scepticism in Robert's face. "I've examined the weather maps. The ocean in its path was unusually warm for this early in the hurricane season. Then, a day out from Miami, the air and water behind it warmed up. I can't explain why."

"Not just unusual. It was unnatural," Jake replied.

"If you're right, how did they do it?"

Jake shrugged. "I think it's got something to do with two satellites."

"I remember they spent the earth on making and launching their own. I thought they were mad, but perhaps there was something more going on." He paused to take a deep breath. "You wouldn't necessarily have to input a huge amount of energy to interfere with a weather system. It's a matter of delivering the right trigger at the right spot and the right time. But that's not the end of it. Messing with conditions in one place will lead to all sorts of unexpected changes down the line. A country that controls its own weather will control the weather of lots of other countries as well. If you engineer a warm wet climate – fantastic for growing crops – for yourself, and the country next door gets a drought and famine, they're going to be seriously angry. They'll think you're stealing their water. That way, rainfall becomes the new oil: worth fighting over."

Robert's words made sense to Jake. Even if Castleton weren't trying to sell their methodology to the military, weather wars were still in the offing. He'd already witnessed the roots of conflict. To save Miami or South Korea, neither Gordon nor Brian seemed concerned about the damage that would be inflicted on Cuba or North Korea. Even so, Jake still recognised the benefit in putting an end to droughts, shunting storms away from people, and alleviating flooding. "It's hard to say what's a knock-on effect and what would've happened anyway," he said.

"True. It's like a midfield player, about to pass the ball to someone on the right wing. He changes his mind, dummies, and passes it out to the left. What are the knock-on effects of that? You can't tell. Once he's put the play out to the left, you can't rerun the exact situation to find out what would have happened if he'd gone the other way. But a really good weather model like your dad's can predict the weather for three days and get it more or less spot-on. That means someone could compare what should have happened with what really happens after they attempt to interfere – though it's not totally foolproof."

Jake decided to raise the stakes. "But what if Castleton's thinking of using the weather as a weapon?"

Robert almost gasped. "Are they? Is that what they're saying?"

The phone rang and, with a sigh, he picked up the receiver. "Hello? Robert Goodhart speaking." He listened for a few seconds and then said, "I'm sorry, but can I call you back? You see, I'm in an important meeting here." His caller talked for half a minute and then Robert said, "Yes. I'll be – I don't know – about quarter of an hour. OK? Good. Speak to you soon." He looked at Jake and said, "Sorry about that. It's a miracle we've only had one interruption. Anyway, *is* Castleton trying to turn storms into military hardware?"

"I don't know for sure, but I'm going to find out."

"Oh? How?"

"I thought you might have some ideas."

Robert stared out of the window and let out a long breath. "Well, there's one thing that occurs to me. You'll need to know what went into Castleton's satellites. I think I know which business supplied the parts and put them together. I can make a few enquiries, I suppose. Can't you access Castleton's computer records?"

"Not the important ones. They're voice-activated and I don't have an important enough voice."

"What about Carly – your mum?"

"I don't think she's important enough either. Anyway, she's never believed the war stuff," Jake answered.

"It's down to you then, Jake. You could refuse to cooperate with Castleton unless they tell you what's going on. Or you could foul up the system by feeding in wrong information. But to do that, you'd have to destroy your reputation for getting it right."

Jake had already thought about that. He didn't want to make deliberate mistakes. He was not sure his self-esteem would let him. And he didn't want to become the next Patmore sorcerer to be sacrificed.

CHAPTER 22

That evening, when Jake told Aidan all about his mum's security system at Castleton and set him the challenge of cracking it, Aidan's eyes lit up. "That's clever. Really clever. You've got to say the time and date as well as your name. So, you can't just record someone logging on and play it back to the computer to hijack their identity – the time'll be wrong."

"But I've got to get in there and find out if – and why – Castleton's making storms," Jake whispered as if someone might be listening, even though they were sitting alone in Aidan's bedroom. "If I log on as Brian Mosby, the computer will let me see all sorts of documents, especially ones about satellites."

"OK. We need to nick his voice and work a few tricks on it. I could . . . er . . . borrow a high-quality microphone for the workstation you're using and it'll record anyone in the room . . ."

"Won't he see it?"

"Unlikely," Aidan replied. "It's tiny. You just plug it in at the back of the computer and it'll store any noise as a sound file. You can save it on a memory card you shove in a USB port. That way, you can walk out with it. I can do some mixing in the studio, or on your PC if I copy some extra software onto it."

"Not at my place. Mum might . . . you know."

"In the studio, then. Our computer downstairs isn't up to it."

"But how do we get the right time and date?"

"Haven't you heard of pick 'n' mix? His name, the year and month are no problem. Record him logging on and we've got them – at least till the end of the month. But you'll have to catch him saying whichever day you want to gatecrash his computer. Then, I can mix it in like a sample. So far, easy-peasy. But then comes the tough bit: patching numbers in to make him say the right time and date."

Jake sighed wearily. The task seemed to fall somewhere between complicated and impossible.

But Aidan was upbeat. "Talk to him. Try and make him say as many numbers as you can. That way, I stand a chance of mixing something that sounds good. Then you'll have to play the sound file at the exact time on the right day. If you miss it by a minute, chance gone."

Nearer to impossible than complicated. But Jake was determined. "When can you get me the microphone?"

"They'll open the studio first thing in the morning. No sense in messing about. I'll swipe it before school. You can have it before you go to Castleton."

*

169

Jake had thought it through. As soon as he was left on his own, he got down on his hands and knees and placed a Biro partly under the terminal. Then, taking a deep breath, he took the memory card – smaller than his forefinger – and, reaching round to the back of the workstation, he slotted it into a USB port.

The only sounds were the whirring of fans inside the main processor towers, the air-conditioning, and Jake's breathing. And the heavy thumping of his heart. Sitting up again, he turned on his workstation, logged on, and set up the sound recorder program in the way that Aidan had shown him. Every few seconds, he glanced nervously towards the door. He feared that someone could enter at any moment and catch him bugging the room.

He dropped to his knees again and peered behind the unit to find the input socket that Aidan had described. It would be round, possibly pink, and it would be labelled with "MIC" or an image of a microphone. Extracting the miniature mike from his pocket, Jake pushed it home.

As soon as he'd done it, the door opened and he recognised Brian Mosby by his smart trousers and shoes. Looking up, Jake banged his head on the underside of the desk.

Brian laughed. "What on earth are you doing down there?"

Jake grabbed the Biro and held it up as he got back to

his feet. "Dropped my pen," he explained, hoping that he wasn't reddening too much. Rubbing the top of his head, he plonked himself in front of the monitor and pressed the return key to activate the program.

"I thought for a minute you were praying to Hurakan."

"Who?"

"The Aztec god of wind and lightning."

"Oh."

Brian switched on his terminal and sat down. After it had loaded, he checked the time displayed on the screen and said in a loud voice, "Brian H Mosby, Wednesday twelfth of July, two thousand and six, nine-thirty-one." He hesitated and then turned to Jake. "That reminds me. It's your anniversary. You started on the twelfth of June."

"Doesn't seem that long," Jake replied. Seeing an early opportunity, he added, "Saint Swithin's Day's coming up."

"Fifteenth of July. That's Saturday. What do they say? If it rains on Saint Swithin's Day, it'll rain for the next forty days. Weather records shatter that myth."

Jake couldn't believe his luck – he was scheduled to work on Saturday. Within seconds, his hidden bug should have captured all he needed for Aidan to put together *Brian H Mosby, Saturday fifteenth of July, two thousand and six*. But it was premature to celebrate. The log-on procedure required the time of day. If he was going to fool the computer on Saturday morning into thinking that he was Brian, he'd have to do it when he was working alone. How could he predict when he'd be left on his own? Even if he thought of a way, how could he get Brian to say out loud the numbers that Aidan would need to assemble the right time?

"Folklore's not always as daft as you might think," Brian was saying. *"Red sky at night, shepherds' delight; red sky in the morning, shepherds' warning.* That intense red colour's down to haze and dust in lazy air. We get our weather from the west, so red sky at night – when the sun's setting in the west – means calm conditions are moving in. A red sunrise means the calm air mass is moving away to the east."

"My grandad says, 'If the moon rises haloed round, soon you'll tread on deluged ground.'"

"Easy," Brian said at once. "Moonlight makes a halo when it comes through cirrostratus or altostratus, and they mark the advancing edge of a warm-front rain belt."

"When high clouds and low in different paths go, be sure that they show it'll soon rain and blow. It was one of the first things I noticed about the sky when I was little," Jake said. "When clouds at different heights go in different directions, it's time to grab a coat."

Brian smiled and nodded. "Wind shear, ahead of a storm. Anyway," he said, "I can see what you're doing. You're keeping me talking."

172

Jake swallowed. That's exactly what he was doing. He froze in his chair.

"But your diversionary tactics won't succeed. Come on. Less chat, more work."

Trying to keep his sigh of relief to himself, Jake relaxed. "Is the computer showing any sign of learning from me?"

"I wish I could tell you it's wised up and you're redundant, but . . . not yet. It can't get to grips with your sixth sense. Human intuition doesn't compute."

Aidan had booked some time in the sound studio after school hours on Thursday. Avoiding Erika Ray, the boys slipped into the studio and straight away Aidan got to work on converting *Brian H Mosby, Wednesday twelfth of July, two thousand and six* into *Brian H Mosby, Saturday fifteenth of July, two thousand and six*. He clipped the *Saturday* and *fifteenth of July* out of Brian's conversation about Saint Swithin's Day and substituted it where he needed it. Then he turned his attention to the time.

"Is nine-thirty-one OK?" Aidan asked. "Mosby said that so it's easy-peasy to drop it in."

Jake shrugged and sighed. "I don't know. That time in the morning, I might be on my own but more than likely Brian'll be with me."

"I'll make it anyway. And a copy that I can put a different time on. I've got an idea," Aidan muttered. "He said *to* lots of times. T-O sounds the same as T-W-O so I can get a *two* from *moving away to the east*, *get to grips*, or whatever. Then I snip *forty* out of *it'll rain for forty days* and you've got a believable two-forty."

"But it's a twenty-four hour clock. That'd be in the middle of the night."

"Ah. In that case, you won't be interested in four-forty either."

"Ten-forty would be good," said Jake. "We take a break at about half-past ten. Maybe I could come up with an excuse to carry on working while Brian's having his coffee."

"No good," Aidan replied. "He didn't say *ten*. I don't think so, anyway." Listening to the sound file yet again, Aidan said, "Hang on. Listen to this bit."

That intense red colour's down to haze and dust.

Jake frowned. "Yeah. So what?"

"It might work," Aidan said.

"What might?"

"He said *intense*. If I chop the *in* and *se* off, you're left with *ten*." He turned to Jake with a grin. "I'll copy it and give you three different versions: nine-thirty-one, ten-thirty-one, and ten-forty. That's your lot."

CHAPTER 23

Saint Swithin's Day arrived, wrapped in a dull cloud-scape. A warm cumulus containing five million litres of water was suspended over Sheffield. Within the rain-storm's nursery, tiny droplets of water jostled as they drifted aloft on the updraught. The bigger droplets chased the smaller ones, absorbing them and growing all of the time. After about half an hour, they became too large to stay airborne. Their weight dragged them down faster than the updraught blew them higher. Evolving into fully-fledged raindrops, they fell out of the saturated cloud and down to Earth.

Last night, Jake had researched weather folklore. At least, he'd explored the tip of the iceberg. Grandad Patmore would have been able to recite hundreds of traditional sayings, but he wasn't easy to contact. Instead, Jake had used the Internet. He'd chosen one particular legend to memorise because he intended to use it as an excuse to carry on working through coffee break at Castleton. While he showered and dressed, he rehearsed the excuse in his head.

Over breakfast, Carly announced that Neisha had

phoned. She'd decided to go into work and, because of the horrible weather, she had offered Jake a lift. "You were in the shower so I accepted on your behalf. You don't want a second shower outside. She'll be here in half an hour. A bit less, maybe."

Jake was suspicious. He guessed that Neisha knew all of Castleton's sordid secrets. Far more than Mum, no doubt. And now, on the day of his most audacious assault on those secrets, she was coming to collect him.

"Good of her, isn't it?" his mum prompted.

With his mouth conveniently full of cereal and milk, he nodded.

When Jake dashed down the sodden path to Neisha's waiting car, the memory card in his pocket seemed to weigh him down even though it was as light as a pound coin. The mobile disk contained a tiny sound file with a ghostly voice saying, "Brian H Mosby, Saturday fifteenth of July, two thousand and six, nine-thirty-one." He also had two backups that he could use in the morning break. If Jake missed all three windows of opportunity, or if the computer refused to recognise the voice, he would lose his chance to sneak into the restricted parts of Castleton's computer.

As he clambered into the car, he was ambushed by the irrational fear that Neisha could see through his cagoule and trouser pocket and into that little memory chip. He was scared that his scheme was just as transparent.

"Hiya," she said brightly. "You wouldn't want to walk in this. And they don't allow dripping in the computer room."

"Thanks," he mumbled.

She looked in her mirror and then pulled away. "How's it going?"

"Good," he answered.

"You're a star, you know. Worth every penny we're putting into your trust." She indicated, turned, and quickly glanced at her passenger. "There's another reason for picking you up. Not just the weather."

"Oh?"

"Yes. Erika's feeling a bit low. You know. To be blunt, she thinks you've been avoiding her this week. I don't like to intrude – and I wouldn't normally – but we know each other pretty well. Is there a problem, Jake?"

Hypnotically, the wipers brushed aside the rain that smudged the windscreen.

He ducked out of venting his real feelings. Instead of crying, "She betrayed me – and so did you," he said, "With this job, there's not much time for hanging out any more."

Again, Neisha looked askance at him for a moment. This time, there was disbelief in her expression.

They hardly said another word to each other for the rest of the short journey.

*

He didn't have a good morning. First, Brian arrived promptly at five-past nine, ruining Jake's first sound file for logging on. Unable to concentrate, Jake's mind drifted away from the isobars, humidity and rainfall patterns. He was too preoccupied.

Brian stood up. "Come on," he said, looking at his watch. "We need a break. You're below par today."

It was 10:24, according to the computer. Seven minutes to go.

Jake got up and walked with him towards the door but, on the point of leaving, he came to an abrupt halt.

"What's up?" asked Brian.

"I just remembered. I was going to check something out for my grandad."

"Sorry?"

"If Candlemas Day be fair and bright, winter will have another flight; but if Candlemas Day brings cloud and rain, winter is gone and won't come again. I promised to see if there's anything in it. I'll miss break so it doesn't cut into work time. Is that all right?"

"When's Candlemas Day?"

"Second of February."

Brian shrugged. "Sounds like junk to me but, if you want to waste your own time, be my guest. I need a coffee."

"Thanks," said Jake, heading back to his workstation.

As soon as the door closed, Jake allowed himself four

minutes of searching his dad's computer for records following a fair-weather 2 February. He had to have some evidence that he'd looked into the legend by the time that Brian returned. Then, at 10:29, he shut down his workstation, plugged in his mobile memory and rebooted the system, making sure that the speakers were turned on. He looked around as if a tornado were bearing down on him, but there was nothing.

When he entered Brian's user name, the computer prompted him to log on. It was exactly 10:31. Throwing caution to the winds, he double-clicked on the sound file that Aidan had called BM1031. Eerily, Brian's voice filtered into the room.

At once, the computer responded with a message on screen. *Say again.*

Jake cursed silently. He'd never seen it do that before. Quickly, before the digital clock moved on to 10:32, he played the sound clip again.

But the computer was not fooled by the synthesised sound. *Voice not recognised.*

Muttering under his breath, Jake logged on as himself instead. He refused to give up. He'd put in a few more minutes of research on the weather around Candlemas Day and then try again with the final sound file: BM1040. It was risky because, if it worked, it didn't leave much time. Brian always took his coffee to his office and made a few phone calls before he returned to the computer room, but he usually got back before eleven.

Jake was too edgy to concentrate on the weather records for early February but he absorbed enough to make a sensible response if and when Brian asked him what he'd discovered. Then he signed out.

His fingers, poised over the keypad at 10:39, were trembling and his breathing was shallow and fast. He knew he was skating on thin ice, but he had no choice. The minute seemed to take an age to pass. When the computer finally went to 10:40, he tried again. *Brian H Mosby, Saturday fifteenth of July, two thousand and six, ten-forty.*

Say again.

Jake played the sound file once more.

Then it happened. *Welcome, Dr Brian Mosby.*

Jake stopped himself crying out in celebration. He glanced towards the door and then double-clicked straight away on the icon for the weather satellite CC3. This time the system granted him access. Immediately, he got a status list. Scanning down it, there were the usual atmosphere-monitoring functions but one odd entry caught his eye.

Mirror: passive mode.

He clicked on the line and the computer responded with further operational information.

Steerable mirror is reflecting sunlight away from the planet surface. CHANGE STATUS.

Satellite not linked to CC4. CHANGE STATUS.

Target not selected. CHANGE STATUS.

Start and end time. SELECT.

An idea began to form in Jake's mind but he couldn't afford to linger. He thought that he had used up enough of his precious time as an impostor on the satellite so he quit the program. He hoped that Brian was not sitting in front of a workstation in another part of the building. The network surely wouldn't allow two Brian Mosbys to log on at the same time from two different locations.

Deciding that CC4 would probably be much the same as CC3, Jake did not try to access it. Instead, he looked around the desktop for documents that did not appear on his own display. The immediately obvious ones were called *WMT May2006* and *Indra*. Jake shook his head. He hadn't heard of Indra before.

He looked at the time in the bottom right of the screen. 10:45. He would have to switch back to his own identity very soon.

But he couldn't backtrack without seeing more of the confidential WMT report that he'd glimpsed in a grey folder three weeks ago. When he opened the document, he could not fail to note the beginning. Two references to *Patmore* leaped out at him.

ABSTRACT. Technological advances in meteorology and demands for more precise weather information by multinational businesses and society have led to the identification of the major variables that affect weather.

181

Improvements in computing capability, modelling techniques and atmospheric tracking (mainly through the work of Craig Patmore) have given us an accurate and reliable method for forecasting . . .

. . . The team also requires a recruit with an in-depth understanding of the global weather network and an appreciation of the effects of adding energy or chemicals at particular times. Having assessed all available information on Jake Patmore, we conclude that his skills would enhance the WMT significantly.

He had no time to be horrified, but he wondered how Castleton had come by all this information on him. His mum? Erika and Neisha Ray? It certainly wasn't something they got from his dad's letter. Trying to put it out of his mind for now, he scrolled to the end of the document.

CONCLUSION. Achieving a versatile environmental modification (ENMOD) capability in the next three years will require overcoming some challenging but not insurmountable technological and legal hurdles.

We have made significant recent improvements in several areas. (a) New seeding particles in water-and-ice clouds have increased precipitation by prolonging the duration of the rainmaking process. (b) Airborne microscopic computer particles (nanorobots), communicating with each other and with the controlling supercomputer, will offer the possibility of creating weather systems. They have navigation capability in three dimensions and may be assembled to make clouds with a wide range of properties. They can generate sufficient electrical potential in the atmosphere to initiate accurately targeted and timed lightning strikes. Additionally, they may be designed to block enemy surveillance methods such as optical sensors. (c) Field tests of our sunlight redirection and focusing scheme have shown it to be a highly effective weather-modification and weather-creation tool.

In summary, we are well placed to capitalise on our technological dominance for modifying battlefield weather through storm enhancement or triggering. However, to realise our huge market potential, we must combine our superior computing power and atmosphere control with inspirational input on the precise effects of any weather intervention.

In the longer term, we should assess modification of ocean currents, manipulating polar icecaps, and opening of holes (skylights) in the atmosphere. We should develop a super-heater aimed at the ionosphere with the aim of exploding the atmosphere outwards (skybusting), altering upper-atmosphere wind patterns, disrupting enemy communications, confusing incoming missiles with unexpected drag forces, and modifying the environment.

Skimming over it, he didn't take in every detail, but he was horrified by the references to battlefield applications and by the apparent scope of Castleton's capabilities. He was also stung by the time. 10:52. Brian could stroll in at any moment.

Closing the file, he made a quick decision about the document called *Indra*. He did not attempt to open and explore it, but his need for answers overcame the sheer panic that he was about to get caught. He dragged its icon to the mobile-drive symbol and copied the file. He was certain that his shirt would be damp with the sweat that was rolling freely down his back. His face was probably flushed red as well. Yet he also felt strangely protected within this cockpit created by his father. It was as if Dad was willing him on, as if Dad's ghost could delay Brian Mosby until Jake had finished his undercover espionage.

As soon as the workstation completed the task, he shut it down and then scrabbled behind it to pocket his flash card. Reloading the computer seemed to take an age. It didn't, of course. It took exactly the same time as always, less than a minute. But it wasn't fast enough.

CHAPTER 24

Before Jake could complete the logging-on procedure, Brian returned. He took one look at Jake and said, "What's up? You look bunkered."

Jake could not disguise the fact that his workstation had been shut down because he still had to speak his name, date and time. "Um . . . I am," he said. "I was getting lots of stuff on February weather and it crashed."

"Really?" Brian looked puzzled. "That's unusual. Not unheard-of, but unusual. Is it behaving now?"

Jake recited, "Jake Patmore, Saturday fifteenth of July, two thousand and six, ten-fifty-six." In a few seconds, the computer was back in action. He shrugged. "Seems fine."

"I'll get a technician to check it over after you go," Brian replied, taking the seat in front of his own monitor. "And what about Candlemas Day?"

"Come and have a look if you want. The weather in the rest of February doesn't have anything to do with conditions on the second. It's not statistically significant, according to the computer."

Brian smiled. "As I said, junk."

The encyclopaedia on Jake's home computer defined Indra at once. He was a Hindu god of the sky, shown as a four-armed man on a white elephant. He unleashed rain and hurled thunderbolts. He was also a god of warriors and nature.

Castleton's *Indra* was just as fearsome. The file described the WMT's first attempt at modifying a storm on a grand scale. It was a simple squall that started life in the South Atlantic. It couldn't be described as a tropical storm because the seawater was too cold. According to the report, only two weak tropical storms had ever hit southern Brazil in the forty years that satellites had been recording weather conditions. But, after Castleton had somehow used its technology to turn up the heat in its vicinity, the thunderstorm raised its game. It could not be called a hurricane either, because it was in the wrong place. Genuine hurricanes fed off sun-warmed tropical ocean water. Yet, when the storm struck the coast of southern Brazil, damaging thousands of homes and killing three people, it looked and felt like the real thing. It had high winds, rain, and an eye at its centre. The press described it as a freak hurricane and blamed global warming.

The report did not state the purpose of Operation Indra. Unfortunately, it didn't provide Jake with written proof that Castleton Computing had tested a weapon. It was plain to him, though, that Gordon Dell wanted to be another god of thunderstorms and warriors.

The document did not express any regret for the damage and deaths. Rather, it revelled in a job well done. It ended with a recommendation that the WMT should use the same technique to experiment with the next storms to form off the west coast of Africa. It also made the point that there was a missing element: control over the *path* of a weather system.

Jake screwed up his face in disgust and his skin went cold. He deduced that Castleton hadn't created Alberto but almost certainly it had souped up the Senegal storms that spawned the hurricane. He also deduced that he was the missing element, brought in to direct storms like a conductor leading the musicians in an orchestra.

Outside, RoboMow was trundling around the garden, cutting the lawn as it went. It had learned the position of Jake's weather station, the flowerbeds, fences and patio. It went up to each obstacle, stopped before hitting any of them, and then went into reverse. Swivelling, it headed off in another direction like a miniature military tank on a search and destroy mission. Whenever RoboMow sensed that it needed charging, it lumbered over to its docking station by the kitchen wall and drank electricity until, refreshed, it was ready for action again.

Everything came together in Jake's mind when Robert Goodhart telephoned. "I didn't find out a lot," the university lecturer said, "but Castleton made two satellites for low Earth orbit. The only remarkable thing about them is that they both have huge flexible mirrors that unfold in space. They were designed to be manoeuvrable and to work in sync with each other. The only thing I can come up with is that they deflect and focus sunshine onto a target on the Earth's surface."

"That's what I think as well," Jake replied. "Do you remember a freak hurricane in Brazil a few weeks back?"

"Yes. It couldn't have been a hurricane, though."

"Castleton beefed it up by warming the air and water around it. Would these mirrors be enough to do that?"

"I would have thought so," Robert replied. "Atlanta absorbs so much of the sun's rays in the day that the city can trigger thunderstorms when it lets go of the warmth at night. And haven't you ever set fire to paper by focusing sunlight on it with a magnifying glass? It's solar heating, made to order. Dangerous."

"What are you going to do about it?" asked Jake, hoping that the academic intended to do something.

"I remember, years ago, playing a couple of rounds of golf with Brian Mosby. He was pretty good. Perhaps it's time I challenged him again. And reminded him that the weather's too big a weapon for human hands."

"You won't mention my name, will you?"

"No," Robert answered. "I'll keep you out of it."

Tin Can lolled on the carpet. As a robot, TC never felt weary and strained but sometimes he mimicked a tired and tense expression. Considering his canine character, he also looked uncannily like a cat that had just guzzled the cream.

Jake put down the receiver and said, "Now we're getting somewhere. I just wish I'd found something that proves they stole Dad's letter." He put a hand on TC's head. "When Castleton people look skywards, they're thinking about a couple of funny satellites, not God. Not God with a capital G anyway. Indra, maybe."

Aidan liked being in the house alone or with Jake but, as soon as his mother walked in, he hated the place. He didn't need looking after. He detested her rules and her concern. He looked again at Jake and said, "Are you sure you want to get her in on this?"

Jake nodded. "Your mum could write an article about Castleton murdering Brazilians with a storm." He held up the mobile disk and added, "I've got proof. Not proof they were turning it into a weapon but proof they stirred it up."

"What'll that do, an article in Mum's rag?"

Jake shrugged. "Bad publicity. Maybe someone in Brazil will sue them or something. They'll have to stop."

"We don't need Mum. I'd rather we failed on our own than use her and succeed."

"She's all right. And I don't want to fail."

Aidan let out a long sigh. "OK. It's your show, I suppose." He led the way downstairs.

Yet Mrs Webb was having none of it. "It's really interesting . . . horrifying. But there's a problem, Jake. It's not a signed copy on official Castleton notepaper. Do you see what I mean?"

Jake shook his head.

Mrs Webb smiled at him. "I'm not doubting you for a minute, but look at it from my editor's point of view – or a reader's. Anyone with a grudge against Castleton Computing could have made this up and typed it into a computer so it looked like an authentic report. And the paper's stance is always sympathetic to local employers."

"Oh, Mum," Aidan cried. "You always spoil everything."

"That's not true, Aidan. It's difficult enough for the paper, working in temporary offices, without you . . ." She took a breath and then said to Jake, "Look, I'm on your side, but have you got anything to confirm it's real?"

"No."

"Jake works there and he says that's what's going on," Aidan retorted.

"Anything *independent*," Mrs Webb stressed. "That's

what the editor would need – the say-so of someone else."

Jake looked down at the flash card in his hand. "No," he said. "There's no one else. Just me." His big idea had proved to be as short-lived as a rainbow.

Gordon Dell was angry. Really angry. "No calls, no interruptions, nothing," he barked down the line at his secretary on Saturday afternoon. Then he turned to Brian and Neisha. "Right. I'm eating into your precious weekend because Jake Patmore's becoming an embarrassment. Can we throw him overboard yet?"

Brian shook his head. "He's too valuable."

"Sure?"

"Certain. We can modify storms without him, but not control where they go."

"OK. This technician who checked his computer. She's one hundred per cent, is she?"

"Yes," Brian answered. "I logged on – apparently – when I was nowhere near a terminal. Somehow, Jake pretended to be me. He must have recorded my voice."

"It still shouldn't have been possible," Gordon replied heatedly.

"No. He must have done some clever editing. You've got to admire—"

"No, I haven't," Gordon retorted. "He's a nuisance. Repeat – a big nuisance. Following in his dad's footsteps." Agitated, he ran his fingers through his hair.

"He got into the latest WMT report and one of the satellite status files. He didn't open *Indra* but obviously he knows about it. As if things weren't bad enough, that means he took a copy of it."

Brian nodded.

"He's a fifteen-year-old, running rings round us!"

"I've put him through a hundred-odd simulations now," said Brian. "So far, the supercomputer hasn't duplicated his knack, but it's not a bad platform to learn from. We won't need him much longer."

"But we've got to keep him onside till we've sewn up the American deal. When the money comes through, we're not so much promoted as catapulted into the big league. Nothing gets in the way of that."

Brian replied, "The cash injection will let us buy more computing power. Then the model will learn faster and we can dispense with Jake's input sooner."

"Quite right. But, don't forget, when the money rolls in, we start paying off the loan on the satellites." Gordon sat back, hands behind his head and said, "So, that leaves just one more security issue."

Neisha agreed. "The phone call."

"Exactly," Gordon replied. "Who did he talk to about the mirrors?"

Brian said, "That's easy. Robert Goodhart up at the university."

"Why do you say that?"

"Before we took Jake on, he was working with

Goodhart. Jake probably thinks of him as a neutral academic in all this. A father-figure."

"You're looking smug. What else do you know?"

"Well, for the first time in ages, Goodhart called me and asked if I wanted a game of golf tomorrow afternoon. Quite a coincidence."

"All right," Gordon said. "Talk to him and find out if it was him on the phone with Jake. If it was, over to you, Neisha. It's your area. You fix it. Two things. Deal with Robert Goodhart and make sure the *Indra* file doesn't go any further than Jake Patmore. Put a lid on all this."

CHAPTER 25

Carly held out her hand. "Neisha tells me you've taken something from work."

Next to Jake, the robotic dog looked sheepish.

"It was just a document I wanted to read."

"A confidential document," his mum replied. "I've got to give it back to Neisha."

Jake fished around in his pocket for the memory card and then surrendered it.

Carly shook her head. "When you started at Castleton, you signed a secrecy clause, you know. What you've done's illegal. The company could take you to court for theft and breach of contract."

Jake hadn't thought of that. But he tried to keep his mind on *Indra*. "You ought to read it, Mum. It'll tell you Dad was on the right lines."

Carly paused for a moment. She lowered her head, gazing at TC, and then looked again at her son. "I'm not going to read it. If you'd nicked a mobile phone, that'd be like me making a few calls with it. It's receiving stolen goods." She asked, "Have you made any copies?"

"No."

"Have you given copies to anyone else?"

"No."

"Why did you pinch it?"

"You said Dad had some weird ideas about power over the weather. Not so weird, according to that file."

"All right, Jake. You're bound to be curious, working where he did, and being like him, but there's a limit. Breaking into the computer by impersonating someone else – aided and abetted by Aidan, I guess – is well beyond the limit. Clever, but not clever enough, because you got caught."

Jake frowned. "How?"

"How? Does it matter?"

"Yes. To me it does."

"Neisha said an engineer spotted it when she was servicing the computer you use. Anyway, you're lucky they're not sacking you outright. Gordon's giving you a get-out-of-jail-free card."

"Just read the file, Mum. Please."

"I can't afford to lose my job. It's got to go straight back to Neisha."

Jake let out a groan.

Tomorrow, he could refuse to work for Castleton any more. But that would be like giving up before reaching the finishing line. To stand any chance of getting that independent proof, he needed to remain a mole on the inside. He was thinking of two different things. He wanted proof that the company was manipulating the weather – especially the South Atlantic storm – and, more important, that they were doing it for military gain. Same technology, very different purposes. The rainmaking that would help a dry country feed its people was the same technique that would weaken a wet country by drowning its army in mud.

As for giving him another chance, Gordon Dell and Brian Mosby didn't have an option. Maybe they would have sacked him if they could master the weather without him. But they couldn't. Each time they meddled with the atmosphere, they let a ferocious dog off its leash and it ran wild. For now, Jake was their only chance of training it to obey commands.

If he thought that walking away from the job would stop them enlisting nature's serial killer for their own ends, he'd do it. But he was sure they'd carry on with experiments like the Brazilian storm and Hurricane Alberto. Without him, there'd be more accidents, more deaths. He could walk away – with principles intact – only after he'd figured out how to stop them.

On Monday, when Gordon reminded him of his obligations to the company, Jake felt as if he were standing before a headteacher.

"We give you responsibilities as an employee, Jake, and reward you well. Very well, in fact. We pay you to play on our side. Let me put it another way. You come to me with a music CD and I buy it from you. That means it's mine. You wouldn't expect to walk off with it once you've been paid for it, would you? Well, that goes for your work here as well. I pay you for it and you don't walk off with things the company owns. Got that?"

Jake nodded.

"OK. That's your warning. If there's a repeat, you get the red card. Understand?"

"Yes."

"Right. The matter's closed. Except that security will now frisk you every time you leave work so don't even think about memory cards, CDs or even papers." He jerked his head towards the door. "For now, back to work."

It was a familiar voice on the phone in the evening. But there was an unfamiliar tone to it. Timo Scarpa sounded gutted. He said, "Have you heard?"

"What?" Jake asked. "A tornado? I didn't see—"

"No. I didn't know whether to call you, but I thought I'd better break the news if you didn't know already."

"Know what?"

"About Robert Goodhart. Apparently, he was playing a round of golf yesterday. But, on his way home, he had an accident."

Jake was shaking. "An accident?"

"There's a road through a wood. He swerved off it for some reason and hit a tree. The police say something must have run out in front of him, a deer or some other animal maybe."

"How is he?"

Timo hesitated before replying, "I'm sorry, Jake. He was a colleague and a friend to both of us."

Jake did not answer. He was thinking of his dad. He was thinking of the parallels. His dad and Robert Goodhart had both turned against Castleton. They'd both been outdoors and had not returned, much to the company's benefit. Jake could not help wondering if the woodland animal on the road was actually a lifelike Castleton robot. He was also remembering what Robert had said to him about Castleton. "You could foul up the system by feeding in wrong information. But to do that, you'd have to destroy your reputation for getting it right." Perhaps Robert had a point. Perhaps it was time to make deliberate mistakes after all. If Robert could sacrifice his life, Jake could sacrifice his self-esteem.

Feeling numb, he went downstairs to tell his mum.

Looking shocked, she stammered, "Are you sure?"

Jake nodded.

"He was . . . a nice chap. He was good to you. And it was . . . what? . . . less than a month ago he was right here in this room." She let out a long breath. "But, before you imagine all sorts, Jake, let me say I've never been a great believer in conspiracy theories, as you know. I just don't think the world's that exciting. It's full of coincidences and mundane tragedies like car accidents and stumbles down hillsides. Not many of them turn out to be conspiracies. It's just . . . sad."

"But what you don't know is, Robert was playing golf with Brian Mosby so he could check out something about Castleton's weather satellites."

"What?" his mum exclaimed.

"When I told him they were messing with the weather – trying to make it a weapon – he believed me. Not like you."

"Jake!"

"It's true."

"I wish I'd never let you sign on at work. All this has blown up since you started."

"But you did," Jake muttered, "and I'm finding a lot of things out."

"You *are* like your dad."

"Good!" Jake charged back upstairs.

TC was left looking agitated.

Breathing heavily, Brian closed his eyes. Neisha certainly knew how to put a lid firmly in place. Dr Goodhart's death made him think about Craig Patmore as well. He hoped that the great man's accident did not also bear Neisha's signature.

The need for secrecy – the necessity of covering their tracks – was all in the name of profit. For Brian, though, it was different. Of course, he looked forward to becoming very rich. He couldn't deny that. But there was something more important to him. The weather had always enthralled him and now he was on the point of mastering it. That would place him among the most powerful people on Earth.

He gazed across the terminal at Craig's son and said, "That's your fifth attempt to nudge this hypothetical hurricane and . . . nothing." He held up his hand to stop the boy interrupting. "I know. I don't feel good either. He was my tutor. One minute we were on the fairway, the next . . ." He sighed. "Let's call it a day. We both need a break."

Today, Jake was in danger of training the weather model to fail. Brian did not believe that Jake was doing it deliberately, though. He looked genuinely distressed and subdued. And he was avoiding all eye contact. Dr Goodhart's death was probably putting him off his swing.

"Brian?" Jake said.

"Yeah?"

"You admired my dad, didn't you?"

"Sure did," Brian answered with a smile. "He had two children. I took one – the computer model – under my wing when I got this job. I didn't know then that I'd get the other one as well a few years down the line."

Jake didn't respond immediately. He appeared to be summoning up the courage first. Then he muttered, "He wouldn't have backed what you're doing with either."

Open-mouthed, smarting at the boy's comment, Brian watched Jake stride out of the computer room.

Home early, Jake watched the ever-changing weather patterns on his monitor. There wasn't much happening in the north of Britain. Typical of high summer, the strong westerlies had given way to significant southerlies bringing hot continental air. All the action was over the Bristol Channel where wind shear made the clouds rotate in an unstable atmosphere. The strong updraft created a tall narrow tornado, 700 metres high. In its twenty-minute life over the sea, the waterspout sucked moisture way up into the sky. On land, people were being pelted with hail, rain and the occasional fish.

For really mean storms that made Bristol's waterspout look comical, Jake turned to America. A brutal sun had heated the Gulf of Mexico, generating warm wet winds that had stampeded north. They met cold dry air over Dallas and there the atmosphere became a cloud factory.

Jake read Timo's urgent email. *Severe weather alert near Dallas. The tornado sirens are about to be sounded. What do you think?*

Jake saw all of the elements that went to make a tornado but something told him that the jet streams overhead would act as a cap, putting a brake on the thunderstorms' spin. He replied, *Forget it. Thunder and lightning, yes. Hail and wind as well. But no tornadoes.*

He looked down at his vigilant guard dog and said, "Watching my every move again?" Jake smiled and shook his head. "Why do I talk to you so much? It's not as if you understand anything. I guess it's because Dad's not here and Mum doesn't believe a word I say. At least you're a good listener."

At once, a cold shiver engulfed Jake's body. At once, he understood.

CHAPTER 26

Jake knelt back to front on the sofa, his elbows on its upright, peering out of the front window. As soon as his mum pulled into the small drive, he told TC to stay in the living room and dashed out to open the garage door for her.

Looking pleasantly surprised, Carly stopped the car and squeezed out of it. "Well, thank you—"

Jake interrupted. "TC hears everything, doesn't he? He's got a microphone."

"Yes," his mum answered with a puzzled frown. "He doesn't understand sentences, just simple orders like *lock doors* and *stay*. He's trained to recognise tone and body language, that's all. You know all this."

"He can see."

"He's got low-resolution digital video: seeing of a sort. He uses it for visual recognition of you and me, friends and family. And smoke and flames. He can smell as well. He's got an artificial nose for sniffing the products of burning. Don't forget he's a walking fire detector as well as guard dog." She put her hand on her son's shoulder. "Let's go in. It's more comfortable than the garage."

Jake shook his head. "No! We've got to talk here. Who sees what he sees and hears what he hears?"

"What do you mean? No one. And, before you ask, he doesn't store a lot of pictures because it's too heavy on memory. Why do you want to know?"

Jake ignored his mum's question. "But could he send a signal to someone else so *they* can record everything?"

"In principle, yes. He'd just need a transmitter."

"Has he got one?"

"Not another conspiracy theory! No," Carly replied firmly.

"Can you take him to bits and find out if anyone's put one in?"

"Jake. You're getting paranoid. What's all this about?"

"Can you?" he repeated.

"I could, but it's not worth it."

"Mum. How did Castleton know I'd copied the Indra file?"

Carly said, "I told you. It was a computer technician who picked up on it."

"How? She could get a list of the files I'd opened at work. It's a doddle. Even I could do that. But how would she know what's been copied to what?"

"There must be a way."

"More likely, someone at Castleton was listening to me talking to Robert Goodhart on the phone here at home – when TC was the only one around."

204

"I've had a hard day at work, Jake, then shopping. I'm tired, hungry and thirsty."

"The weather-modification report said they'd assessed all available information on me. Where did it come from? How did they know I was a weather prophet?"

"Let's talk about this inside."

"With TC listening? No!"

"If you could just hear yourself, Jake. It's . . . ridiculous."

Jake couldn't tell her the main reason he was convinced that Tin Can had been the traitor all along. Not without letting on about Dad's letter. Its disappearance made total sense to Jake if the pretend-dog was a sophisticated bug. When Jake had folded the letter into a book on his bedroom shelf, TC had been watching. The robot could have been beaming low-resolution camcorder images back to Castleton Computing. During her next visit, Neisha Ray could have said she was going to the loo and nipped into Jake's bedroom instead. Guided by TC's pictures, she would have known where to look for the letter.

And what did all this make Erika? It made her innocent. She wasn't an actress after all. It was her mum who was playing a role. Neisha was putting on the perfect performance as a friend to the Patmores.

As soon as Jake thought of Erika, though, an idea formed in his mind. To stand a chance of making it work, he would not be able to kick up a fuss about the treacherous Tin Can. He'd also have to abandon Robert's idea of making deliberate mistakes to sabotage the training of the weather model. He turned to his mum and shrugged, "You're probably right. Never mind. It's just me being silly."

Carly shook her head and grinned at the abrupt U-turn. "You always were a funny lad. And I do love you, even if I don't always show it. Come on," she said, "help me with the shopping. Then we'll get dinner. You're doing the chips."

Outside the shops after school hours, Erika looked from one lad to the other. Settling on Jake, she said, "I'm honoured. Fancy little old me being granted an audience with the two of you."

Jake did not expect anything other than sarcasm, resentment and hostility. That's what he deserved. He did not try to lie his way out of the situation by telling her he'd been too busy to see her. "I'm sorry," he said. "Really sorry. I thought you were ... you know ... telling your mum secrets about me."

"Like what?"

"You knew Mrs Webb was going to send me a Castleton file – till it got blasted by lightning. And I told you I was getting paid by three insurance companies."

Arms tightly and indignantly folded across her

midriff, Erika replied, "You told me not to tell Mum, so I didn't."

"But she found out, and so did Castleton, so I thought . . . Well . . ."

Aidan chipped in, "Seemed like an open and shut case."

"Well, you were wrong. Both of you," she retorted.

"Sorry," Jake repeated.

"Now you're trying to make it up to me. Why?"

"Because . . . it's the right thing to do."

Erika tossed her hair over her shoulder and then folded her arms again, putting on a cold front. "What are you after?"

"Well, there is something . . ."

Erika butted in. "So, you're saying sorry to butter me up. That's all."

"No." Offended, Jake's reply came out louder than he intended. "I really am . . ."

"Save your breath," she muttered before walking away in a showy huff.

Hands on hips, Aidan watched her go. "Well, that's that. It's down to you and me."

"It would've been better with Erika."

"Maybe," Aidan replied. "But are you really sure about her?"

Erika halted at the newsagent's, turned and then stomped back. "Hey. I know what you're going to say behind my back: I'm ignoring you because I don't believe your apology. But that'd be like sinking to your level. You kept away from me because you didn't trust me."

Aidan glanced at Jake and said, "We hadn't thought of that."

"Well, that's boys for you. You ought to try thinking sometimes."

"So, have you changed your mind?"

She nodded. "You'd better count me in, I guess."

Beaming, Jake said, "Brilliant."

There was still not a glimmer of a smile on Erika's face. "And you'd better tell me what we're up to."

As quickly as he could, Jake told her everything he'd learned about Castleton Computing. Then he said, "Now you know why I've got to stop them. I might be able to if I had access to all their weather-modification tools. I could really screw things up. But they'd have to trust me more to give me clearance."

"And how are you going to make them trust you?"

Jake smiled. "You and Aidan have got to persuade me – with TC listening – that the world needs a new weapon: the weather. I've got to change my opinion and agree with it."

Erika seemed hesitant. She frowned. "I'm not sure I can do that. I'm no actress."

"No, I know that now," Jake replied. "Anyway, we'll plan it out before we do it. We can't write it down and read from pieces of paper, though, because TC will be spying as well as listening."

"But we can rehearse our lines as much as you like." Looking pleased with himself, Aidan added, "We'll call it brainstorming. Get it? Easy-peasy."

"And, to make sure Castleton get the message," Jake said to Erika, "you go home afterwards and tell your mum I've seen the light."

"Mum," Erika muttered.

Jake nodded. "OK?"

"You think my mum's behind all this stuff, don't you?"

"Well . . ." Not wanting to be too blunt, Jake left his sentence hanging in midair.

"I'll have to think about it."

Erika shivered pleasantly at the tickling sensation on her neck. Chewy had run up her arm and was nestling on her shoulder. The rat's fur was brushing against her bare skin. She knew that rats had a terrible reputation, of course, but she loved her own. Chewy wasn't loathsome, dirty or disloyal. But there again, Chewy didn't live in the sewers.

Erika's mum was exactly the same as her friends' mums. Overprotective, critical and annoying. Never short of cutting comments about binge drinking, staying out late, make-up, short skirts and spangly tops. Erika had once caught her rummaging through her schoolbag, looking for cigarettes, drugs and contraceptives. That had led to a gigantic fight about trust – or lack of it. Erika simply didn't feel attached to her mother. If Jake said she was acting as a spy for Castleton Computing, she felt inclined to believe him. After all, Jake was OK – in a screwy sort of way.

And her mother had never been subtle when it came to Jake Patmore. Short of pinning a *Suitable Boyfriend* sign on him and attaching him to her with handcuffs, Mum had made it very plain that she approved of Jake. That was one reason why Erika had resisted. But her curiosity and interest in him had refused to go away, despite her mum's endorsement.

Now, Erika was caught in a dilemma. She still needed her mum; she needed a home and money. And it was Erika's right to slag off her own mum. But she wasn't so sure about Jake and Aidan putting the boot in. Yet any outrage she felt about the accusations flying in her mother's direction didn't last long.

Erika took Chewy in both hands. "I've decided," she said quietly to her pet. "I'm going to go along with Jake if only because it'll give mum a chance to prove she's not the bad guy. If she is . . ." Erika shrugged. "She deserves what she gets, I suppose."

CHAPTER 27

Jake's miraculous conversion took place in his bedroom on Thursday evening, when Aidan and Erika had just one school day left before the summer holiday. TC stood in the middle of the room, turning from Jake to Aidan to Erika in turn. The toy traitor looked confused yet earnest.

Erika bent down and tapped the dog's back. Wandering off script, she whispered, "You're cute, aren't you?"

Jake said, "Well, I don't know . . ."

"He is," Erika insisted.

"No. I meant what Aidan was saying about blasting countries with hurricanes."

"Hey. Don't knock it. That's how my mum makes a living. And it's got its uses. Like, if terrorists are hiding in some mountains – that's the in place for terrorists to hang out – you could give them the worst winter ever. Come spring – and the big thaw – you go and collect the bodies. Easy – and risk-free. Well, risk-free for the good guys."

"I'll give you that one," Jake replied.

"It's better than wars going nuclear," Aidan put in. "At least the weather's natural. Not like radioactive fallout."

"True," Erika added. "And better than any missile or chemical attack because it doesn't pollute, does it?"

"There is that," said Jake, "but it's not *replacing* bombs and stuff. It's *adding* to the weapons stockpile."

"Who says?" Erika replied. "It might replace nuclear bombs. That's got to be good."

Tin Can turned to Jake expectantly.

Jake shrugged and sighed. Then he muttered, "Maybe."

"It won't be every country that can make a storm or fiddle with rain," Aidan said. "It's not going to turn into a world war."

"America and Russia have got enough atomic bombs to wipe out the entire world," Erika argued. "You can't do that with the weather. You'd just make it a bit windier, wetter or whatever."

"All right, all right," Jake said, putting up both arms in surrender. "I get the message. You think Castleton's doing a good job and I should join in."

"People are always going to fight," Aidan replied, "and there are worse weapons than the weather."

"You're not to blame anyway," Erika added. "If you worked for a place that made guns, you wouldn't be banged up if anyone got shot with them, would you? You didn't pull the trigger."

"OK," said Jake. "Point made. Maybe it's not such a bad thing, working for Castleton."

Looking relieved, Tin Can buckled his back legs to sit down.

Neisha Ray loved her job. She had been the first to recognise the threat posed by an out-of-control Craig Patmore. She had also been the first to think of placing a transmitter secretly in Tin Can during a routine service so she could monitor young Jake's weather-forecasting skills directly. Now, the bug served a second purpose: to find out if the son was becoming as unstable and dangerous as the father. Neisha also stayed close to Carly so she could keep tabs on her thinking and reassure her that nothing untoward was happening in Castleton. And Neisha had one final tactic. In the hope of keeping a finger on the pulse of the Patmore family, she had encouraged Erika to befriend Jake.

When Erika came in, she shut the door too loudly as always.

"Hey. Just been to Jake's."

"You two are back on talking terms, then? That's good."

"Been talking about you – work, anyway."

"Really?"

"Uh-huh. He's had a change of heart."

"What do you mean?"

"You owe me a favour. He was wondering whether he should quit, but me and Aidan convinced him Castleton's OK."

"Thanks very much," Neisha replied with more than a touch of cynicism. "What was his problem?" She'd heard Erika's conversation with Jake and Aidan but it was natural to ask.

"He thought you shouldn't be using storms in – what do you call it? – defence or something."

"He shouldn't be talking about that. Neither should you."

Erika shrugged. "No big deal. It won't go any further. He was just . . . working it out in his head. We all need to talk things through sometimes. Anyway, he's behind Castleton all the way now. Thanks to me."

Neisha smiled. "No need to milk it, miss. Your allowance is staying exactly where it is."

"Huh. No gratitude." She tramped upstairs to her room where her pet rat waited.

Jake felt soiled and angry. For years he'd had private conversations with TC, his substitute imaginary friend. Now he knew that everything he'd said had been relayed to Castleton. Every time he'd expressed his inner feelings and desires, every time he'd confessed some naughtiness, every time he'd said something about his dad, girls, his mum, the weather, and school, someone had been listening. Gordon Dell, Neisha Ray and the rest must know him better than anyone else on the planet. Jake could not begin to recall all of the thoughts that he'd shared with Tin Can – and with Castleton. Yet it struck him that he'd said lots about Erika and how much he fancied her. He was mortified because he'd passed private verdicts on her face, legs, hair, her clothes, her brain and body without knowing that her mother could hear every word.

Sure, he was horrified by Castleton's abuse of the weather but it was more than that now. The bosses had committed two personal insults as well. They'd stolen his dad's letter and stripped him of his secrets. To say he felt defiled and bad-tempered was putting it very mildly under the circumstances.

He hated Gordon Dell and his business. He hated Castleton's agenda. Most of all, he hated Neisha Ray because she was two-faced. Despite appearances, she was no friend of the family, just like TC. Right now, though, Jake had to hide his feelings. He had to carry on as if he'd never figured out Tin Can's double role. He had to act normally until he'd finished what his dad had set out to do. Jake had to work for Castleton until he could ruin it.

CHAPTER 28

Almost a week into the summer holiday and he was still working full-time, still trying to teach an old weather model new tricks.

The head of the WMT looked across at his young colleague and sighed deeply. "I'm fed up with this. I can't pretend you didn't see *Indra* and our report. You did. And I can't pretend you don't know all about our satellites 3 and 4."

"So?"

The ice broken, Brian said, "So, we might as well talk about it."

Jake shrugged as if he didn't care one way or the other.

"I never did congratulate your initiative. Company policy's stern displeasure. But logging on as me was clever. A birdie if ever I saw one." Brian smiled. "Anyway, since you got caught and told off by the boss, your attitude's been top-hole. I'm changing your security level. You're not getting open access to the system but there's no point excluding you from things you know." He paused before adding, "You said your dad wouldn't have backed what we're doing. That hurt."

"He developed this," Jake replied, waving towards the bank of processors, "to stop bad weather causing havoc. He didn't do it to aim storms at people on purpose." Jake realised that Brian would have known his dad's attitude if he'd seen the letter. Perhaps he hadn't. "But I've thought about it some more."

"And your opinion's different?"

Jake remembered one of Mr Cosgrove's Geography lessons on the climate. Organising a debate on global warming, Cosmic had asked Jake to take on the role of oil tycoon. His task was to persuade everyone else that global warming wasn't happening at all. If that didn't work, he had to change tactics and convince the class that climate change had nothing whatsoever to do with the burning of oil-based fuels. There'd been no winners and no losers, Cosmic had concluded at the end, but Jake had gained experience at role-playing. He needed it now to argue in favour of something he opposed. "It's just nature, isn't it? Not like other weapons. It'd be great if you could put bombs out of work. And if we're going to save people by nudging hurricanes away from places like Miami, someone's always going to use the same idea to steer them at a target. It's the other side of the same coin."

While he spoke, Jake recalled Timo's word-image of a big twister: the most frightening and unstoppable

217

thing on Earth. He had a picture in his mind of the woman whose car was picked up and hurtled through a brick wall into someone's bedroom. He saw photographs of a line of mangled homes. And, worst of all, he envisaged the smart missile of the weather world sandblasting skin from its victims' bodies.

"That's right," Brian answered. "It's our job to discover what's possible. It's the politicians' job to ban anything they don't like. But the Ministry of Defence knows our game plan and there's no sign of them shutting us down. Quite the opposite. We've had government grants and all sorts."

"Mum programs military robots and spy planes, so I don't see why I can't work on weather modification," Jake said. "Besides, I'm good at it."

Brian nodded and grinned. "You certainly are."

Elbows on his knees, chin resting on his fists, Jake gazed at TC. "Castleton's like having all-day Geography and Geography's the only good bit at school."

When the bedroom door opened a crack, TC became alert at once and turned towards it.

But it was only Mum. "Downstairs," she ordered.

Understanding the command, Tin Can began his laboured walk to the landing, ready to negotiate the staircase.

"You too," she said to Jake.

"When's dinner?" Jake asked.

Carly shrugged. "Whenever you make it, I guess. I don't feel like cooking." She showed him a tiny flash card and then whispered, "I'm going to give TC a new chip to add to his programming. After that, we'll go out for a meal."

"OK."

In the living room, Carly instructed TC to stand still. Then she said in a clear loud voice, "Deactivate security devices." Crouching down, she opened a small panel in his left side.

To Jake, it was like watching a surgical operation – without the blood.

Next to the green LED, indicating that TC was powered up, there was a red light. Carly looked up at Jake and said, "That means all his defence mechanisms have shut down. I don't want him attacking me because he feels under threat."

"I thought he could never attack you or me."

"True. It's a precaution, in case of accidents, like turning off a light before changing the bulb." She slotted the new chip into one of his input ports, closed the wound in his side, and stood up again. "Done." Facing TC, she commanded, "Restart all systems." Then she smiled. "There. That wasn't so painful, was it? Now, stay."

To Jake, she said, "Come on. I want to show you something."

Jake followed her to the bedroom-cum-study where

she established a radio link between her computer and TC. "What's going on?" asked Jake.

Quietly, she replied, "This new chip'll give me a list of all devices in him. See? Microphone, security modes, laser, contact sensors, fire-detection systems, electric-shock capacitor, movement detectors, all sorts." When she scrolled to the end of the list, she caught her breath, turning visibly pale.

"What's up?"

"There's a greyed out item."

"So?"

"That means I can't click on it. I don't have any control over it."

Jake grimaced. "What is it?"

"I don't know. It's greyed out."

Mother and son stared at each other for a moment. Then Carly said, "Time for us to go out for a meal – without TC."

CHAPTER 29

Carly looked up at the waiter as if he were a spy for Castleton Computing. Without a word, she waited for him to deliver the starter and then she leaned over the table towards Jake. In a hush, she said, "I owe you an apology."

"Oh?"

"Gordon admitted he was changing the weather, but it's more than that, isn't it? I've been thinking. And I decided to take a look at that *Indra* file . . ."

"But I thought you'd given it straight back!"

"After your heartfelt plea, I couldn't resist making a copy first. I opened it yesterday. I think I owe your dad an apology as well. It's . . . er . . . It's a bit late." She broke off the conversation and picked up her spoon but didn't tuck into the soup.

Jake's relief was massive. Someone other than Aidan and Erika believed him.

Carly shook her head. "*Indra*, Dr Goodhart, and now something – a transmitter, if you're right – in TC." Mechanically, she sipped the soup, probably not even noticing the taste. After two spoonfuls, she paused again. "Years ago, when your dad was alive, I was testing robot programs and I had this prototype for TC. A dog on wheels, if you like. Not very dog-like or sophisticated. But really stable, bigger and more powerful than TC, and much easier to program than anything with legs." She put the spoon down. "After your dad's accident, when I got back to work, all my programming had been set back to default values. I didn't worry about it – I had other things on my mind – but I never got an explanation."

"Why's it important?"

"Well, it was as if someone had used the robot for something and then wiped its memory, as if I wasn't supposed to know about it."

Jake looked puzzled for several seconds while the unwelcome idea penetrated his brain. Then he nodded. "You mean, like pushing someone over an edge?"

Carly shrugged. But she didn't deny that it was on her mind. "I checked all our current robots and one – a small bipedal, could be mistaken for a child at a glance – was set to default the Sunday before last. Strange it was a Sunday – and straight after Dr Goodhart had his accident."

"What are we going to do, Mum?"

"After this," she replied, glancing down at her soup, "we're going to see your grandad. Grandad Patmore."

There was no answer to their knock at the front door

but they found him standing as still as a statue in his back garden. "Hello, Grandad," Jake said brightly. "It's me and Mum."

"Shh," he said without even glancing at his visitors. "You'll frighten him."

"Who? What?"

"The hedgehog. See?" He pointed to a brown bundle of spikes that was lumbering awkwardly like a robot across the bed at the bottom of the garden.

"Flea-ridden things," Carly muttered.

"No. They're good for gardens. You want hedgehogs. They eat slugs." When the ungainly creature disappeared under a bush, Grandad turned towards them. The peak of his cap kept the sunlight out of his eyes. "You'll be wanting mugs of tea."

Much to Jake's surprise, and before Grandad could escape to the kitchen, Carly opened her arms and flung them round him. Hugging him fiercely, she convulsed with sobs. Between sniffs, she muttered, "You were right about Craig all along."

"So," he said, stroking her hair with thick and grimy fingers, "it's taken you nine years to figure it out, eh? Your company killed that daft husband of yours. Fell down a hill? He were pushed."

"Sorry, Dad," she struggled to say.

He held her at arm's length by her shoulders and gazed into her face. "What now, love? Are you asking me what to do about it?"

She wiped her eyes and cheeks with her hand. "First, I had to let you know. I don't have any sort of proof . . ."

"Proof?" The old man laughed and shook his head. "You science types! Come on. Tea." Waiting for the water to boil, he said, "You don't need proof. You just need to open your eyes." He nodded towards Jake and said to Carly, "He knows." Then Grandad put his foot in it. He looked at Jake and said, "They stole your dad's letter, didn't they?"

Carly stared open-mouthed at Grandad Patmore and then at Jake. "Letter? What letter?"

Jake closed his eyes and groaned inwardly. "Um. Well . . ."

Over tea, the whole story of the secret letter came out. At least his mum didn't explode with resentment. Perhaps Grandad's presence restrained her. More likely, she really did understand that Jake would want to keep a bit of his father to himself. Even so, when Jake finished, his cheeks were flushed red.

Grandad said to Carly, "So, don't come to me asking what to do. First, ask who stole the letter."

Carly did not utter a word. She didn't need to. Her doubts about Neisha were written across her silent face.

Grandad waited for her to think things through before adding, "Ask Jake what to do. He knows best." The elderly weather prophet put down his empty mug and announced, "It's going to rain. Didn't you see the cows on the farm? When cows slap their sides with their tails, it's a sign of rain."

Jake nodded in agreement. In humid weather, flies always plagued cows. He pointed to the east.

Grandad smiled. "That's right. It'll be with us for a while. *When the rain is from the east, it lasts a day or two at least.*" Then, his head dropped. He was perhaps thinking about a downpour that had brought floods to York many years ago.

As soon as Carly swung the car round, put her foot down and made for home, she asked, "What *are* we going to do, then?"

Jake looked at his mum but she kept her eyes on the road. He thought that driving was her excuse not to make eye contact. "Not much," he answered. "Just carry on as normal until I can get far enough into Dad's weather model to do what he started to do."

"And what's that?"

"Sabotage it so they can't use it as a weapon."

Carly sighed. "That's what he was up to just before he died."

Jake had never thought of himself as brave. His one skill was deciphering the sky. But he could put on a show of confidence to calm his mum's nerves. He said, "I'll be careful."

"It's no use trying to persuade you to do something safer, is it?"

225

"No."

"Thought not. I don't like it one bit. I'll step in if I get the slightest whiff of trouble," said Carly. "You're not going to end up like your dad."

"No."

"In the meantime, I guess I can't fiddle around with TC or tackle Neisha. Or try and get your dad's letter back."

"No. That'd tell them we're on to them. Then they'll shut me out of the system for good. But . . ."

"What?"

"You know your logging on program? Voice recognition."

"The one that's *almost* secure."

"Yes," Jake replied. "It'd be handy if it could be bypassed."

"It can't."

"It can't *now*," Jake said, "but maybe in a few days?"

Carly glanced at him, sniffed and shook her head wryly. "You're becoming devious in your old age. I'll see if I can create a backdoor without anyone noticing."

"That'd be good."

Jake felt quite nauseous but happy. His mood was a result of tension, the coming risks, and a rare togetherness with his mother. "You know," he said tentatively, "you were always in a good mood. I thought you didn't care about him any more."

His mum's cheerless expression turned into an uncertain smile. "No. I still care, Jake. But I need a break from the grieving widow. Underneath, he's still there. And so is the pain."

"There you are," Brian said pleasantly, presenting Neisha with a mug of coffee. "As it comes. Black, no sugar."

"Thanks. How's it going with Jake Patmore?"

"Not a tap-in yet, but I can see the flagstick."

"You what?"

Brian smiled. "We're getting there. The computer's showing signs of learning. It's still nowhere near as fast as Jake, but its calculation time's down by a factor of three." Brian sat down carefully, making sure he didn't spill his drink. "You knew Craig Patmore, didn't you?"

"Mm." She took a sip of hot coffee.

"What was he like? Did you get on with him?"

"Yeah. He was fine. Good-looking, too. Passionate about work, the weather, Carly and his kid. Nothing else."

"He didn't play golf, then."

Neisha smiled. "Not as far as I know."

"So, he didn't have his accident on the way back from a golf course."

Neisha froze with the mug halfway to her lips. Staring at Brian, she said sternly, "Everyone knows exactly how he died. Including you. He went out to

227

measure the guts of a storm and a freak wind got the better of him." She looked down at her mug and then back at Brian. "If he had to go, he would've wanted to bow out doing something he loved."

Brian shrugged. "With a six-year-old boy, I doubt he'd want to bow out at all." Then he added, "Don't get me wrong. I'm happy as long as I can watch the weather and improve my handicap, but . . . that round of golf with my old lecturer was a bit bizarre. Coming up to the fourth hole, he starts lecturing me. It's like being back at university. You know. The weather's nature's way of trying to balance heat, humidity and pressure around the globe. Hot tropical air rises and makes for the poles. Warm equatorial water goes the same way. And what drives all this? Not Castleton, he says, not satellites with state-of-the-art mirrors, but the sun." Brian slurped his coffee and then carried on. "The Earth's spin and the haphazard layout of land and sea have their wilful way with air circulation but humans – Castleton employees included – don't have a part to play. That was the gist of his sermon. We're too puny to understand it fully and we'd only mess it up. And he said it without once mentioning Jake Patmore. Still, it meant he wasn't concentrating on his game. He bogied the fourth and fifth."

"What's your point, Brian?" Neisha said rather impatiently.

"While Robert's digging himself out of the rough on

the thirteenth – unlucky – I report it all to Gordon and then, straight after the game, Robert's taken out of the picture. Lid slammed down."

"We can't dictate when a deer's going to run out in front of a car, Brian."

"To be honest, I'm not much bothered, but my guess is you didn't use a deer," Brian replied indifferently. "Just like you didn't use a stiff breeze on Craig Patmore."

CHAPTER 30

For Jake, it had gone beyond finding a separate source of information on the Castleton warmongers to convince the local press. Besides, the only other company contact who would vouch for his story was hardly independent. His mum's say-so wouldn't be enough for Mrs Webb and the editor. Anyway, an article in the paper wasn't top of Jake's priorities right now. He was too angry to be satisfied merely by inflicting bad publicity.

For a change, Jake and Brian Mosby were huddled in front of the same terminal. They were looking at an Ordnance Survey map of the High Peaks to the west and north of Sheffield, with atmospheric pressure, temperature and wind readings superimposed on the view. "It's basic Geography," Brian was saying. "Bread and butter to you. If we focus sunlight on a lake, it'll evaporate a lot of water and heat the air. The warm wet air will climb, especially if it's shunted uphill on the prevailing wind, and turn into cloud. Ideal for making a rainstorm. Or turning an existing small storm into quite a big one."

Jake nodded. Pointing at Broomhead Reservoir, he said, "Let's do it here. The wind's southwesterly so it'll send clouds up the slope. Bolsterstone and Stocksbridge will get drenched. Again."

It had rained constantly over the weekend and Monday, just as Grandad and Jake had predicted. Now, in a harmless lesson, Jake was following it up with an artificial shower. He felt like those wizards in olden times who used to burn magic dust to gain control over rain. The supercomputer had replaced enchantment.

"Well, that's the theory," Brian replied. "It won't take long to make a local rainstorm. I've got solar panels on my roof and, on a sunny day like this, they get up to 150 Celsius before you know it – way hotter than boiling water. And that's without focusing the sun's rays. Our satellite mirrors are much more efficient." Clearly proud of the technology, he smiled and said, "Heavenly."

Brian double-clicked on the CC3 icon and scrolled down the list until he reached the entry that read, *Mirror: passive mode*. He clicked on the line to open the control functions.

Steerable mirror is reflecting sunlight away from the planet surface.

He positioned the pointer over the *CHANGE STATUS* box and activated the system. At once, the supercomputer responded with, *You are about to position*

the steerable mirror to reflect sunlight onto the planet sur-
face. CONTINUE?

Brian continued. *Satellite not linked to CC4. CHANGE STATUS.* Again, he proceeded with the setting-up. After a few seconds' delay, the system told him: *CC3 linked to CC4 for maximum focus. Target not selected. CHANGE STATUS.*

"Right," he said. "Here's the crucial bit. You don't want to mess this up. You can type the coordinates in, but that's longwinded and it's too easy to make a mistake." He brought up the map again, saying, "It's better to pinpoint the target with the mouse and double-click on it. Like so."

After Brian had selected the spot, the map disappeared and, after a few moments, the satellite program splashed a message across the screen. *These coordinates identify Broomhead Reservoir, South Yorkshire, UK. Focused sunlight will cause intense heating. Do you wish to continue? ABORT INSTRUCTION/CONTINUE.*

Brian opted for *CONTINUE* and the program asked him to choose the area to be heated. *IRRADIATE ENTIRE FEATURE SELECTED/IRRADIATE 75% OF FEATURE SELECTED/IRRADIATE 50% OF FEATURE SELECTED/IRRADIATE 25% OF FEATURE SELECTED/SPECIFY AREA IN SQUARE METRES CENTRED ON SUPPLIED COORDINATES.*

When Jake looked puzzled, Brian said, "Physics isn't your strong point, is it? Anyway, the mirrors are bendy.

Make them more concave and you can focus the beam really tightly on a few square metres on the surface. Less concave, and you can warm lots of square miles of an ocean. Here, we'll go for seventy-five per cent," he said, "so the edges of the reservoir don't cop it. That way, we won't burn anyone fishing on the bank. But," he added with a grin, "we won't be able to barbeque their catches for them."

Next, he had to pick a start and end time for the operation. He glanced at his watch and said, "Let's turn up the heat in ten minutes. There's no point hanging around."

"All right," Jake replied, fascinated by the process.

To finish, the computer summarised all of the requested parameters on a single page. Brian read through them to check that he was satisfied and then pressed the *return* key. "Up there," he said, glancing towards the ceiling and sky, "the satellites will be talking to each other and rotating into the right position. Like in a sci-fi film. Beautiful. No noise or dramatic music, though."

"What would happen if you picked a target on land?"

Brian shook his head and frowned. "Never done that. It's too risky." Echoing Robert Goodhart's remark on the day before he died, Brian said, "You know what happens when you focus sunlight on paper with a magnifying glass. Things would burst into flame." He leaned over the keypad and tapped in fresh commands. "Let's see what a conventional weather satellite is making of the conditions near the reservoir. I'll zoom in and monitor temperature and cloud cover. We should start to see thickening cloud pretty quickly."

He was right. A rain cloud soon gathered over the village of Bolsterstone and spread to the town of Stocksbridge beyond. Jake watched, intrigued by the efficiency of Castleton's invention. Yet he was also distracted. He could not stop his eyes wandering over the map to Green Moor on the other side of Stocksbridge. That was where his dad had fallen to his death.

"Good, isn't it?" Brian said. "Of course, I can't let you loose on it. Company policy, you understand. But that's how it works. With this, you're a god."

Brian looked thrilled and Jake did his best to disguise his distaste.

Thinking about his options for scoring a hit against Castleton, Jake asked, "What if we wanted to turn this rain cloud into a thunderstorm and strike something tall with lightning? You can do that, can't you? It was in the WMT report."

"Yes, but it's a bit more complicated. We'd have to lace the cloud with tiny particles called nanorobots. That means we'd have to send a plane up to inject them where we wanted them. Then we could use them to kick-start lightning strikes when and where we wanted them."

Jake's ploy was paying off. He was being treated like a trusted employee. He was finding out a lot of useful information if he ever had the opportunity to turn the weather weapon on itself, but he dismissed the notion of a carefully-aimed lightning strike on Castleton. The nanorobots made it too complicated to be realistic. He might be able to make a thunderstorm and just hope that lightning would hit Castleton because it was the tallest building in the neighbourhood. The devastating electrical surge might strike the air-conditioning unit on the flat roof, travel down the ducts into the computer room, and burn out the weather model, just like lightning had wrecked the main computer in the local press office. Without the controlling nanorobots, though, the idea was too hit and miss. The artificial storm might let loose its thunderbolts somewhere else altogether or it might not discharge any lightning at all. Jake needed a more precise and dangerous plan.

That evening, Jake underwent a second miraculous conversion. It took place in the park opposite the shops with Erika and this time he was transformed from friend to boyfriend. At least, he thought that's what happened. He wasn't certain because he was in uncharted waters.

They were walking and talking when suddenly she came to a halt. She took both his hands in hers, pulled him towards her and kissed him. More shocked than surprised, Jake put his arms around her tentatively and wished that girls, like computers, came with instructions. They stood there, embracing for what seemed to be an age, while one jogger overtook them, an old man hobbled past, and his inquisitive Labrador sniffed their shins. Jake felt sure that Erika would feel him trembling.

She didn't comment on it. Instead, she held his arm, pointed to the sky and said, "Hey, that's nice."

Near the horizon, there was a thin sheet of dappled cloud, glowing bright orange and yellow as the sun dipped down.

"Cirrocumulus. Not that common on their own." Jake readied his new camera.

"Don't tell me. It means it's going to pour."

"No. It must be wet high up, but one on its own means nothing. It's going to be nice for a bit." He positioned himself in front of an oak, ready to take a photo of the silky effect with a silhouette of a bough in the foreground, but stopped. Normally, it never crossed his mind to put people in the frame – that wasn't the point and they'd only spoil the view anyway – but this time he changed his mind. "Why don't you stand under that big branch?" he said, nodding towards it. "That'd be good."

"OK."

His first attempt looked great on the camera's LCD screen so he didn't take a second. The colourful cirrocumulus was a great backdrop to the bough and Erika's head and shoulders. Because her face was partly shaded, she had an air of mystery and her wistful expression was difficult to define.

They walked past the old pavilion where a lot of kids hung out, usually drinking cider and smoking. "Fifteen's a rotten age," Erika said with her eyes on the pavilion. "Too old to do the things that're legal. Too young to do what you want to do. Youth clubs are rubbish, nightclubs won't let you in. Sixteen's all right. You can leave home, quit school, smoke, and all sorts. Like, have sex."

"Um, yeah. You can join the army and drive a moped as well."

Erika squeezed his arm and laughed. "I never saw you much in the pavilion. You don't care about belonging, do you? With you its just the weather."

"That's right."

"I like that about you. Screwy, but you're pretty cool for not caring if you're cool or not."

"Have you got a dad?" Jake sighed at his clumsy question. "Of course you have. I mean, where is he?"

"New Zealand. He said he couldn't stand Mum any more and left. I blamed him at the time but maybe he'd got the right idea. I don't know. I was only little. They say New Zealand's really nice. I'd love to see it – and him – one day."

Jake nodded. "Nice thought."

They strolled back to Erika's house hand in hand. "I don't want to kill off my dad's model really," Jake admitted to her. "It's amazing. But if people can't be trusted with it . . . Dad was going to wreck it so he'd want me to do it now."

At the front door, she got out her key. "He wouldn't want you to get hurt, though."

Jake repeated what he'd said to his mother. "I'll be careful." Then he remained silent until they entered Erika's room. There, he looked at Chewy the rat, and asked, "Why's he called Chewy anyway?"

"She," Erika replied. "She just loves wires. Given half a chance, she'll chew through the lot. She's nearly electrocuted herself twice, chomping through electric cables." Erika took the brown rat in her hand and changed the subject. "How are you going to smash the computer? Take a hammer – or an axe – into work?"

Jake smiled at the absurd thought. "They might just spot an axe on the way in. And I think they'd hear hammering. They'd take me away before I could do much damage. Perhaps I should let Chewy loose inside it. But even that won't work. There's bound to be backup copies of all the programs anyway."

"How, then?"

Jake glanced at her. He was sure that she was on the level. After all, she'd kissed him and hugged him and held his hand. He trusted her. "Well, I'm going to get the satellites to blast the Castleton building . . ."

Grimacing, Erika interrupted. "You said it'd, like, catch fire. That'd do for the computer and any backups all right, but what about all the people inside? Including you. And Mum."

"It's OK. I'll program it to happen on a Sunday morning – this Sunday, with a bit of luck – when it'll be more-or-less empty. I saw Brian run the system. It looks easy enough."

Erika did not reply.

Jake watched her face fall. He guessed that she was thinking about her mum, panicking about what would happen when Neisha didn't have a job. "Sorry, Erika, but . . ."

"Yeah. I know." She took a deep breath. "It's got to be done."

"There's plenty of other jobs your mum could do."

Erika nodded. "Yeah. You're right. But what about you and this Castleton program? They won't let just anyone fiddle with it. And how are you going to do it so they don't find out?"

Jake went quiet for a couple of seconds. "I haven't finished planning it yet."

"Hey. Tell you what you want to do. They won't expect you to use the same trick as last time, pretending to be your boss. They'll think you learned your lesson because you got caught. But I could get Aidan round here to record Mum. You could log on as her."

"Um. Maybe." Jake was hoping that his own mum might come up trumps, but he replied, "Worth a try, I suppose."

CHAPTER 31

Aidan and Erika had not managed to put together a recording of Neisha Ray that was even halfway convincing. They'd run into a brick wall almost straight away. They'd not been able to get her to say her own name. After all, in normal conversations, mothers did not announce their full names to their own daughters. This time, Jake would not be able to log on by pretending to be one of the elite.

Yet his mum had found a way of adding him to the personnel with top-level clearance. So, on Friday afternoon, he was about to make another excuse to stay in the computer room over break.

It was shorts and T-shirt weather but Brian still wore a flash suit. When he walked away from his workstation, he noticed Jake's hesitation and laughed. "What's your grandad said this time? Spit it out. *If the ash is out before the oak, you should expect a thorough soak?*"

Jake shook his head. "Never heard him say that. And I don't know how I'd test it anyway. No. *How many fogs in March you see, that many frosts in May will be.*" He hoped that Brian wouldn't spot the edginess in his voice.

"Easy to check," Brian replied. "Pure statistics. But I'm under orders to make sure you're never left on your own in here."

"Oh." Jake's heart sank.

"But I have to admit, you haven't spoiled your score-card recently . . ."

"Thanks," Jake said too eagerly.

Brian shook his head with a grin. "Just be good. And I'll give you a tenner if March fogs equal May frosts. It's as likely as floods in the Sahara."

Jake was almost shaking with trepidation but he managed to reply, "Can't you arrange that?"

Brian laughed again. "There are limits, you know. And that's way beyond. See you soon."

The closing of the door sounded final, as if Jake had been locked up for life. But he knew that, at any second, one of his jailers could come in to check on him. Despite the air-conditioning, he was sweating pro-fusely when he opened the Control Panel and clicked on *Network Properties* just as his mum had shown him. He selected the Access Control tab and clicked on *User-level access control*. The software told him *This page enables you to specify users who have access to each shared resource.* The list of people with access to the most restricted areas of the supercomputer was called *Priority1*. The document could not be altered by anyone as lowly as Jake. According to his mum, Gordon Dell and Neisha Ray were the only people who could open and modify *Priority1*, so there was no chance of adding Jake to the list of the most trusted individuals in Castleton Computing. But Carly had prepared a little surprise. She had made a new list that did include Jake. She'd called it *Priority1J*.

Normally, the system did not allow any tinkering with Access Control but Carly had permission to suspend normal security for thirty minutes while, in another part of Castleton, she tested improved voice-recognition software for logging on.

Jake highlighted the *Priority1* filename and typed in *Priority1J* instead. Pessimistically, he waited for the computer to reject the new list of trusted users but there was no response. He pressed *OK* and it was done. For at least a few minutes, he would have the same clearance as Brian Mosby.

Glancing at the door, Jake double-clicked on the *CC3* icon and scrolled down the list to locate the entry, *Mirror: passive mode*. He opened the satellite control functions and confirmed that the steerable mirrors were reflecting sunlight away from the Earth. Stage fright brought that horrible sickly feeling back to Jake's stomach as he double-clicked the *CHANGE STATUS* box. Just as it had done for Brian, the supercomputer told him, *You are about to position the steerable mirror to reflect sunlight onto the planet surface. CONTINUE?* He did not linger.

So far, it was going according to plan. Even so, he was

jittery in case someone barged in and caught him red-handed. He feared what the company would do to him – and his mum – if their sabotage were to come to light.

The next step was to link up CC3 and CC4 so that the mirrors would act in sync, reinforcing each other. Jake could hardly believe the power at his command. He was like a puppeteer in reverse. The strings at his fingertips stretched upwards for kilometres. He was orchestrating the satellites' dance in near-space. He understood why it made Brian feel like a god.

The system reported: *CC3 linked to CC4 for maximum focus. Target not selected. CHANGE STATUS.*

It was the crucial bit, according to Brian, and Jake was going to do exactly what his supervisor had never done because it was too dangerous. He restored the map of Sheffield to the screen and zoomed in until he could distinguish individual buildings in the street. Making sure that he'd identified Castleton's premises, he double-clicked on the site. It was like painting a giant crosshair on the felt roof above his head to guide the satellites' deadly aim.

The map melted away and a large red-lettered warning appeared on the screen. *ALERT. You have selected coordinates that correspond to an address on land. Focused sunlight will cause intense heating, fire hazard and lethal effects on personnel. Do you wish to continue? ABORT INSTRUCTION (STRONGLY ADVISED ACTION)/CONTINUE.*

Jake hesitated and checked his watch. He could not afford to waste time on second thoughts, but he wanted to remind himself of Castleton's crimes. He wanted to convince himself all over again that he had right on his side.

If Jake allowed Castleton to pervert the weather, every living thing would be affected because atmospheric conditions influenced all life on land and in water. Through Tin Can, the company had bugged him for years, depriving him of his privacy. Through Tin Can, the company had stolen the only solid connection to his father. And, on top of that, he feared that Castleton had arranged the deaths of his dad and Robert Goodhart. Yes, he would continue with the procedure. He was right to continue. He would not lose his nerve now.

He was faced with another five options. *IRRADIATE ENTIRE FEATURE SELECTED/IRRADIATE 75% OF FEATURE SELECTED/IRRADIATE 50% OF FEATURE SELECTED/IRRADIATE 25% OF FEATURE SELECTED/SPECIFY AREA IN SQUARE METRES CENTRED ON SUPPLIED COORDINATES.* Jake wanted to make sure that the building took a heavy dose of the sun's energy but he didn't want to burn anyone nearby. Remembering how Brian had avoided harming any anglers on the banks of Broomhead Reservoir, Jake selected the 75% option.

To complete the exercise, the computer asked him to

specify a start and end time. He was about to type his responses when the door opened.

His fingers leaped away from the keypad as if it were white hot. His heart seeming to stop, he gasped and nearly jumped out of his seat.

Immediately, his brain fished around madly for some reasonable explanation for fiddling with the secret satellites. But what excuse could he possibly offer? There was no innocent reason.

CHAPTER 32

Carly had every reason to be worried. She'd contrived an opening of the security shutters for half an hour, but she didn't know if Jake was able to take advantage. Worse, she didn't know if he was about to be caught in the act. She left her own laboratory and took the lift to the top floor. There, she padded down the passageway and put her head around the door of the computer room. Jake was on his own, hunched over his terminal. When he jolted upright, he looked as if he'd seen a ghost.

"All right?" she asked.

"Mum!" he said, his voice halfway between a reprimand and a whisper.

Carly looked down the empty corridor and then back inside. "Is it working?"

"Nearly there."

"How much longer?"

Jake shrugged. "A couple of minutes, I guess."

It was clear to her that Jake wanted to be left alone to concentrate. She said in a hush, "I'll hang around outside for five minutes – till you're done. If Brian or whoever comes along, I'll delay them."

"OK," Jake replied, his eyes glued to the monitor again.

She left him to it and went back down the passageway where she pretended to wait for a lift.

Jake was forecasting a weekend of brilliant sunshine. That meant he could select anytime on Sunday for the satellite mirrors to turn the heat on Castleton Computing. In an unending blue sky, the sunlight would not be filtered through cloud. It would be at its most powerful. The roof would probably catch fire in minutes. The supercomputer would fall victim next.

Jake assumed that there would be backup disks of the weather model in case of accidents. To keep it restricted, there wouldn't be a lot of copies. Jake also figured that the software would be too valuable to Castleton and too confidential to be allowed off the premises. If he could destroy the whole site, he'd wipe out the supercomputer and any backups. He hoped to finish it once and for all in the weekend's summer sunshine. Of course, his dad's letter was probably somewhere in the building as well. That would be his sacrifice.

He selected a start time of 11:30 when the sun would be nearing its most intense. He didn't care so much about when to end the exercise, as long as the job got done. He put in 14:00 and then wrapped up the program. He skimmed through the summary that appeared on screen, pressed the *return* key, and it was complete.

Returning at once to the Control Panel and Network Properties, he replaced *Priority1J* with *Priority1*. Then the operating system was back to normal and Jake could breathe again. But it wasn't really normal. Secretly, Jake had his finger on the trigger of a gun that would turn and point at Castleton on Sunday morning.

The tremors in his hands subsiding, Jake assembled facts about fogs in March and frosts in May as quickly as he could. Hoping he was not wearing a guilty expression, he braced himself for Brian's return.

Brian came out of the lift and almost crashed into Carly Patmore. "Oh. Sorry," he muttered.

"My fault," Carly replied. "Just been to see Jake."

Brian nodded.

"I wanted to check with you," she said. "Is he getting on all right now?"

"I've never known anyone to hit so many holes in one. He's one of life's mysteries. And enormously helpful. You must be proud of him." Brian paused and then said, "I was going to ask you about Craig."

"Oh?"

"You don't mind?"

Carly shook her head.

Brian got the impression that she wasn't keen to talk

about Craig but, for some reason, she'd decided not to duck his question. "Was he like Jake?"

"Physically?"

"No. I mean, could he look at a skyscape or satellite chart and feel the weather?"

"No. Craig was all hard work and facts and figures – and computers. Jake's very different. He's all inspiration."

Brian nodded. "It's great to supervise him. I just wish I'd worked with Craig . . ." He sighed and stopped talking. After all, there would have been no job for him at Castleton if Craig had survived. "I'd better get going." He nodded towards the door at the end of the passageway.

Carly looked at her watch and seemed relieved. "Yes. Me too. See you."

As he entered the computer room, Brian said, "Bet I don't have to find my wallet."

Jake smiled weakly. "No. Your tenner's safe. Fogs one month don't match frosts the next."

"Another bit of folklore bites the dust." Before logging back on to the weather model, Brian looked across the table. "The artificial intelligence is on the ball now. It's learning from you. It won't be long. Days, probably."

"Then I'm out of work."

Brian smiled and shook his head firmly. "No chance. We'll still need people who are in touch with the weather. I'd have to speak to Gordon about it, but you've got a job here for the rest of your life if you want it. If you carry on cooperating."

Just before Brian gave the monitor his full attention, he noticed an enigmatic expression on Jake's face. It had vanished before he could interpret it.

Jake could not prevent suspicion flashing across his face. He wondered if Brian's comment was deliberately ironic. Jake might have a job for the rest of his life but maybe Castleton did not expect that to be very long, especially if artificial intelligence was making his intuition redundant. Anyway, after Sunday, it wouldn't matter.

Jake had done all that he could do to thwart Castleton Computing. He had to hope that no one would check the satellite status for the rest of the day. He also had to hope that neither Gordon Dell nor Brian Mosby would come into work tomorrow and delve into the program. Then, on a brilliant Sunday, the weather-making machine would turn on itself. His dad's wishes would finally be realised.

In a way, Jake regretted that he hadn't set the satellites to focus on the building right now. Then, there would not be an opportunity for anyone to discover what he'd done and outmanoeuvre him. But his conscience wouldn't let him. There may not have been enough time for everyone to get out safely.

At six o'clock Jake joined his mum, who was waiting anxiously for him in the reception area. Together they left the premises and walked towards home. Out of sight of Castleton, Carly stopped and grabbed her son's arm. "Well?"

"Done," he replied. "Sunday morning. Eleven-thirty."

Carly didn't let go of him. "It's awful. Have we done the right thing?"

"I think so."

"That's not enough when I'm feeling fragile, Jake."

Jake took a deep breath. "I'm sure it's what Dad . . . you know."

Carly's head drooped. "I guess," she muttered.

CHAPTER 33

Sipping his end-of-the-week wine, Gordon Dell looked like a smooth vampire with a goblet of blood in his hand. "He failed the test. I can't say I'm surprised or disappointed," Gordon said. "It's exactly what I expected, that's all. Jake's turnaround to our way of thinking was way too easy and convenient. Amateur dramatics and transparent tactics." He glanced at Neisha and said, "I realise I'm implicating your Erika too, but it was naive."

"They're teenagers, Gordon," Neisha said.

"So you've told me before. No excuse. And it's not like throwing paper darts when Miss turns her back in Maths. Jake's trying to wreck the place. Or at least he thinks he is. He made the decision to tangle with the heavyweights. No one forced him into it. So, he can't complain when he takes a knock-out punch."

"They acted in front of Tin Can," Neisha said. "That means they've twigged about the transmitter."

"Pity," Gordon replied. "But it was never going to last for ever. It's done the job required."

Brian put down his empty glass. "We're lucky Jake didn't go for an immediate strike on the building."

"Luck didn't come into it," Gordon snapped. "I had his computer monitored every step of the way. Anyway, he never stood a chance of doing any damage because I had a technician make sure he only got into a dummy site. He got to play with virtual satellites, that's all. The real ones weren't compromised at any time. Not by a teenager with ideas above his station. Is he still indispensable to us?"

Brian had got used to having Jake around. He admired the boy as much as his father, but that didn't make him untouchable. "He's given the computer enough pointers to finish its training."

"Good."

"What about Carly?" Neisha asked, wiping a little wine from the corner of her mouth.

"Carly," Gordon repeated. "Good question. We all saw her part. She's decided to bat for the opposition so she can't complain if we bowl a few bouncers at her." Then, changing mood from severe to self-satisfied, he picked up a file of papers from his desk and waved it gleefully. "American signatures on the contract and the Patmores aren't vital to us any more. We deserve a good weekend." He looked at the other two and then said to Neisha, "We certainly deserve another glass of wine. Pour it, will you?"

*

"Everything changes tomorrow," Jake said, his head bowed.

On the platform by Meadowhall Shopping Centre, Erika looked up at the sky. "Like, one of your cold fronts – or whatever they're called – moving in?"

Jake's grin was shallow. "No. The heat wave's with us for two more days. I mean, a different sort of scorcher. A very narrow one."

"I know." She peered down the line at the coming Supertram, her face turning serious. "I wonder what our mums will do. No more Castleton."

"That's not all," said Jake. "Dell will probably work it all out when the building goes up. Or he'll guess."

"He might think it's a normal fire, an accident."

"Not after fire fighters tell him it was hottest on the outside of the roof. He'll know what I did then. He'll work out I know about TC, as well."

"Yeah. But the important bit's your dad's computer stuff. That will have gone. No more screwy storms."

The tram pulled into the terminus and delivered another batch of eager shoppers, bristling with purses, wallets, plastic cards and chequebooks. On each and every face was a look of hunger for goods.

Fingers intertwined, Jake and Erika took a double seat in the tram. "What are you going to do tomorrow?" Erika asked him in a quiet voice. "Stand around and watch?"

Jake shook his head. "Just stay at home."

"Bet you'll be clock-watching, listening for fire engines, and tuning in to local news."

"Maybe. What about you?"

She shrugged. "No idea. I don't know about Mum, what she'll do."

"You could come round to mine. You might need to get out of her way when it all goes up. She might ask you some awkward questions."

"True. I wouldn't fancy that." Erika hesitated and then giggled. "I wouldn't fancy being grilled about a grilling."

Jake barely managed a grin in return.

The morning sun shone fiercely through an unbroken sky. In the garden, Jake could feel the rays burning the skin of his unprotected arms. When he looked at his reddening left forearm, his eyes were drawn to the watch on his wrist. Nearly eleven o'clock.

It was a breathless Sunday. Inside his weather station, the mercury was reaching the 30°C mark. The rain gauge attached to the fencepost was dry and the anemometer cups were becalmed.

The minutes on Jake's digital watch seemed to be as sluggish as the stagnant air. The gap between each passing second seemed to lengthen as the sun climbed higher and shadows shortened.

The slow day had begun ridiculously early. Jake hadn't slept much and he'd woken at dawn when sunlight slapped him across the face. Drenched with sweat, he'd got up, dressed, and padded downstairs. There, Tin Can had greeted him by wagging the metal tube that was his apology for a tail. Jake had gazed at the artificial creature and groaned. Even before breakfast, the appearance of the sun and TC had reminded him of the enormity of the day.

The mobile in his trouser pocket rang and vibrated against his leg. He answered it with a brief, "Yes?"

"Mum's just left for work," Erika said, anxiety clear in her voice.

"She's *what*? You didn't stop her?"

"I tried. No good."

Jake groaned. "I'll get Mum to sort it out."

"All right. Be quick."

Jake shouted to his mother, asking her to come out into the back garden. Shutting the door behind her so that TC could not join them, he gave her the news.

Carly looked aghast as she listened to him. "Neisha's gone into work? She's been a bitch, but she doesn't deserve . . ." She made for the door. "I'll get her on her mobile."

"But don't tell her . . ."

"No. I'll . . . er . . . think of something."

Neisha reached for her phone with her left hand while she continued to operate the mouse with her right. "Oh. Hi, Carly. Everything OK?"

"Yes. Where are you?"

Neisha smiled to herself. "It's a lovely day. I should be on a beach, on holiday, in the garden, anywhere but work."

Carly sounded flustered. "I think you should come round here."

"Why?"

"Because . . . um . . . Erika . . ."

"What about her?" Neisha was puzzled at first, and then anxious. "She's not with you, is she?" Neisha hadn't considered that her own daughter might get involved in the end game. Her right hand froze on the mouse.

"Not at the moment. It's about Erika and Jake. You know."

"Can't it wait, Carly? I can get away after . . . I don't know . . . an hour. Two at the outside."

"Not really. You're going to have to trust me on this one," Carly replied. "It's got to be now."

"Well . . ." The easiest thing would be to agree. If Neisha refused, Carly might upset everything by racing into work in an attempt to rescue her from a non-existent threat. "All right. I need quarter of an hour, then I'll set sail."

"Fine. Just make sure you're here by half past."

"Will do."

Straight away, Neisha called home.

Erika answered, "Hey."

"It's me," Neisha replied. "I want you to do a few things for me."

"I was thinking of going out, maybe calling in on Jake."

"No! I don't want you to. I forgot to put the washing on and water the plants. It's the weather for it. You could do it for a change."

Stroppy, Erika sighed. "What's this about?"

Her daughter's prickliness rubbed off on her. The pressure of dealing with Carly and Jake didn't help either. "It's about you doing a few chores. You're on holiday, I'm at work – on a Sunday."

"You're still at work?" Erika asked, suddenly frantic. "I told you not to go in today!"

"All right, Erika. This is something we need to talk about face to face. This afternoon, I promise. I'm leaving in a couple of minutes."

"Good."

That confirmed it. Her own daughter knew that the Patmores had plotted an attack at eleven-thirty. To protect Erika, Neisha needed her to stay where she was until the whole thing was over. "Right now," she said, "I want you to promise you'll help around the house. Please. Washing, vacuuming, anything really. There's plenty to be getting on with."

"Yeah. All right."

"Good girl. I'll see you soon."

Satisfied, Neisha put the phone down and checked

the time. Turning back to the computer, she clicked on Tin Can's control functions.

Relieved, Erika glanced at her watch and let out a long breath. Her mum was going to be safe. But Erika was suspicious. Her mother seemed very keen that she should stay at home and she didn't know why. She could only guess. And she guessed that it was something to do with Jake. Ignoring her promise, she made for the door.

CHAPTER 34

Eleven-nineteen. Jake was sure that his watch had lost the ability to display the figure 20.

His mum, equally on edge but trying not to show it, said, "You'll wear it out."

"What?"

"Your watch. You're looking at it too much."

"Sorry."

Carly smiled. "I know how you feel. I thought I'd get distracted from dinner, so I've put the roast to come on automatically."

Jake sighed. "I'm not going to feel like eating a big Sunday lunch."

"Why don't you go out and snap a few pictures?" his mum suggested.

Jake screwed up his face. "There's nothing to shoot. It's just one big patch of blue out there. Boring."

Carly was dressed for the weather. Shorts and sleeveless top. "Neisha will be coming soon."

Jake nodded. He didn't want to say any more with TC in the room.

261

Reluctant to settle, Tin Can walked up and down uneasily between them.

Jake's eyes followed the robotic guard dog and pet. TC did more than protect and amuse, of course. Jake's mum used him as a gadget for testing new programs and he was a spy for Castleton. If it weren't such an insult to Erika's Chewy, Jake would have called him a rat. The metallic dog was certainly a guinea pig and a mole. The thought should have amused Jake but today, at eleven-twenty-two, he couldn't raise a smile.

Each second was a drop in the ocean. It barely made an impact on the passage of time. Jake hardly dared to say a word to his mum in case they let something slip in front of the Castleton traitor. But retreating out of TC's range again would have been equally suspicious. So, they said little and nothing of significance.

Fidgety, Carly got to her feet. "I haven't had a coffee yet. It's getting late." She headed for the kitchen with Tin Can lagging behind her.

At least she wasn't cracking open another bottle of wine. Jake guessed that his mum needed to break the tension as much as she needed a drink. Like TC, Jake followed her. He sat at the breakfast table, sunshine powering through the window and baking his already clammy back.

Eleven-twenty-four.

It was obvious that Carly didn't want to think about what would happen in six minutes' time. While she waited for the kettle, she looked out of the other window and said, "There's a pigeon on the lawn. Your grandad would have me shoot it. It needs cutting actually. The lawn, that is. And the weeds are taking over again. There's never enough time. Now you're earning, perhaps we should get a gardener in."

While his mum wittered, steam began to emerge from the kettle's spout. It reminded Jake that the satellites were supposed to be aimed at water where evaporation took away much of the heat so that the surface never reached a critical temperature. On dry land, there was no water vapour to act as a safety valve. The surface would simply get hotter and hotter until it reached its flashpoint. Then it would burst into flame.

TC trundled into the corner of the kitchen. He opened the utility cupboard that had been adapted especially for him, plugged himself into the mains and feasted on electricity.

Outside, a couple of mean magpies scared away the pigeon. "I don't think Grandad Patmore likes magpies much either." When Carly heard the click of the kettle turning itself off, she turned away from the window and made her coffee.

In four minutes, Castleton's satellites would turn themselves on automatically. Then it wouldn't matter what Jake said within Tin Can's hearing. For now, though, he forced himself to talk trivialities. "You could invite Grandad over. He'd do the lawn – and shoot the vermin."

"Yeah, maybe. I doubt if he'd leave his own precious garden, though."

Even when Jake came out with trivial chitchat, he could not help but see haunting parallels. Exterminating vermin reminded him of what he was doing at Castleton.

Carly's eyes drifted to the kitchen clock on the wall. She took a cautious sip of her coffee and then put the mug down. Rummaging in her handbag, she extracted her mobile.

Jake didn't need to be told what was on her mind.

"It's me," she said. "Are you on your way?" She listened to the response and then replied, "Good. See you in five minutes, then." She looked at Jake with relief written on her face. "Neisha's just getting into her car."

Jake let out a long breath. He didn't want to be responsible for Neisha's death, even if she did come close to being vermin.

His watch showed eleven-twenty-nine. The time before the satellites activated was now measured only in seconds. If Neisha Ray had left the premises, it was very unlikely that she – or anyone else – would have long enough to turn on a computer, open the right file and cancel his sabotage.

Both Jake and his mum had run out of small talk. He

stared at the digital countdown on his wrist while she watched the sweep of the kitchen clock's second hand.

At eleven-thirty exactly, they looked at each other in silence. It was an anticlimax, of course. No one blew a whistle, sounded a siren or rang a bell. No drum roll, no explosion, no fireworks. Nothing. It would take a few minutes.

Carly walked to the radio perched on the work surface above the utility cupboard. She was about to turn on the local news when she let out a scream. At first, it was pure shock but, in an instant, it became a reaction to pain. TC had sunk his metallic teeth into her bare leg.

Her screech ended abruptly as Tin Can delivered a powerful electric shock. Carly jolted backwards and threw up her arms involuntarily as if she'd been struck by lightning. Stunned, she collapsed. She was unconscious before she crashed heavily onto the tiles.

Jake cried out, "Mum!" He took a step towards her motionless body but at once a narrow red light came out of TC's side and stung Jake's arm. He yelped and jumped back.

The short blast from the laser was a warning, like a shot across the bows from a warship's cannon. Jake wanted to get down on his knees to help his mum – if she was still alive. He wanted to run out of the back door as fast as he could, leaving Tin Can behind. He wanted to tackle and disable the robot. Yet he did nothing. He did not need to be told twice to stay exactly where he was. He froze by the table.

It took Jake a few seconds to understand what TC was doing. While a movement detector and the laser pointed threateningly at Jake, Tin Can had his head in the cupboard. His jaws were clamped around the piping leading to the gas meter. He was twisting his head little by little to undo the nut that joined the pipe to the meter. As soon as it was slackened, the place would fill with gas. Going cold, Jake realised that the walking fire detector was turning fire starter. TC would explode the gas with his laser or maybe someone would focus sunlight onto the house to ignite it. Either would be as devastating as lighting a match.

Trying to think clearly, Jake said in a trembling voice, "Deactivate security devices."

TC carried on, deaf to Jake's command.

"Deactivate security devices," Jake repeated, almost shouting the command.

Again, nothing. The LED in his side remained green, showing that all of his defence mechanisms were still powered up.

It was natural to blame Tin Can. He had felled Mum and now he was loosening the pipe that would fill the room with flammable gas. Yet TC was just an unthinking machine, carrying out orders. Those instructions had to be coming remotely from Castleton and they were overriding his mum's programming. It was becoming horribly clear to Jake that his attempt to destroy the weather weapon had been discovered and derailed. Like his dad, Jake was being punished for his disloyalty. If Castleton had also sussed out his mum's part in the plot, that would explain why Tin Can had turned on her as well. As far as the company was concerned, both Patmores had outlived their usefulness.

Jake couldn't stand rigidly to attention and wait to be blown apart. But what *could* he do? If he made a run for it, Tin Can would bring him down with a laser. Besides, TC would have probably locked the doors anyway. Jake was trapped.

And what about Mum? She looked dreadfully still and pale. Maybe there was a slight movement of her chest. If she was breathing, the rhythm was far too slow.

Jake detected a faint and ominous hiss. The muted sound soon amplified and the sickening smell of gas wafted over him.

His senses alert, he also caught sight of movement to his right. Turning his head, he saw Erika at the window. She was mouthing, "What's going on?"

Jake did not dare to react. Gas was gushing into the kitchen now. It was in his nose, mouth and lungs. He was tasting it as well as smelling it.

Erika banged madly on the glass.

Hearing the noise she was making, TC stopped working on the pipe and looked around.

That was Jake's cue. At once, he knew what to do. He was certain that Neisha Ray would be operating the remote control. That's why she'd gone into work and not turned up at the house. If she had any sort of compassion left, she'd be horrified that Erika would suffer the same fate as the Patmores if she ordered Tin Can to ignite the gas. Jake had an easy way of telling Neisha that Erika was outside. Trusting that TC's microphone and transmitter were still on, he shouted, "Erika! Open the door. Or smash a window!" Then he yelled her name again to make sure that her mum heard.

Immediately, TC pricked up his artificial ears and looked alert. It was a posture that Jake knew well. The dog's programming did not cover this situation. His artificial intelligence was not telling him what to do, so he was waiting for a command. At the other end of the radio-control, Neisha must have been thrown into confusion. She was figuring out her next move.

Jake shouted at TC, "Unlock doors." But it was no use. Even with Erika tugging on the handle, the back door wasn't budging.

Jake wasn't going to wait. He dodged round his mum, lunged at Tin Can and grabbed the mechanical pet in his arms. Yanking him away from his recharging point, Jake lifted him up in his arms like a real dog. His knees buckled with the weight but he staggered to the sink and, finding strength from somewhere, he hurled TC through the window.

With gas still escaping into the kitchen, Jake knelt by his mother. He wasn't sure if he could drag her limp body to a different room. He wasn't sure if he should. The outside doors were locked so he couldn't get her away from the house.

Then Carly stirred. Her eyes remained closed but she whispered, "Go."

"But . . ."

"Go!" she repeated, more urgently.

Feeling torn, Jake said, "OK. I'll get help."

Leaving her, he clambered onto the draining board and made himself as small as possible.

Standing at the side of the window, Erika shouted, "Be careful!"

Jake was about to fling himself through the hole, between the glass teeth protruding from the frame, when the electric timer turned the gas oven on. The spark lit the cooker and converted the kitchen into a bomb.

CHAPTER 35

Jake didn't remember flying through the broken window and crashing onto the lawn. He didn't remember the overwhelming pressure that sucked all of the air from his chest. He didn't remember Erika ducking down, protected by the brick wall, while the roof and fragments of the kitchen flew over her head. He didn't remember her dashing to his side and shrieking, "Jake. Are you . . .?" He didn't remember seeing his weather station blow apart or TC lying broken and inert.

When Jake opened his eyes, a woman in some sort of uniform was leaning over him. Her voice seemed to be distant, echoing softly in his deadened eardrums. "It's OK. You're going to be fine."

The hospital had patched up his gashes, checked him over and pronounced him free of serious injury. A lot of gas had escaped through the kitchen window so the explosion was not as severe as it might have been, and Jake had been catapulted through the hole in the window rather than through glass. His cuts and bruises were the wounds of someone who had fallen a few metres.

Erika held his hand and said with a smile, "They want your bed for someone who's ill."

His head pounded and he could still feel the foul gas in his aching lungs. He shut his eyes and drifted again.

"What about Mum?" Jake muttered.

The nurse took a deep breath. "I don't know, Jake. It's too early to say. She's in Emergency."

"Can I see her?"

Shaking her head, the nurse said, "Not a good idea at the moment. Let the doctors do what they can for her. When she's stable . . . Anyway, she's in good hands. And so are you," she said, looking at Erika. "But I've got to release you to a responsible adult. You need some rest and then you can come back and see your mum. I'm told there's a friend of the family – Neisha Ray – waiting in reception to take you under her wing."

"No!" Jake cried.

At first, the nurse smiled. She probably thought that his outburst was a drunken after-effect of his trauma. Maybe she expected him to be delirious. Then, looking at him more closely, she realised that he was terrified.

"That's my mum," Erika said. "Believe me, Jake doesn't want to go with her."

"Well, who then? Apparently, your mum's parents are on holiday. The police are trying to get hold of them."

Jake felt miserable. Grandad Patmore wasn't on the

phone. Timo Scarpa was miles away in London. He could think only of Mr Cosgrove. "Cosmic Cosgrove," he muttered.

When the nurse looked puzzled, Erika explained, "Our Geography teacher."

"Funny name. What's his number?"

Jake and Erika looked at each other and shrugged.

"I know," Erika said, suddenly upbeat. "Aidan's mum, Mrs Webb. Bet you know her number."

Jake did, yes. But somehow his confused brain couldn't recall it. "They're in the telephone book," he told the nurse. "Carter Knowle Road."

"All right," she said. "You wait here. I'll go and sort it out."

As soon as she disappeared from view, Jake and Erika glanced at each other. "You know the problem with going to Aidan, don't you?" Erika said softly. "Mum knows all about him. She knows where he lives."

They didn't need to say any more to each other. They took off down the corridor, away from the reception area, away from Neisha. They emerged from a fire exit, opposite the Physiotherapy Department. There, a patient had just clambered out of a taxi.

"Can you take us somewhere?" Erika asked the driver.

"If you've got the fare."

Neither of them had much money.

Jake's head was still sore. It felt twice its normal weight and half as fast. He said, "I know. West Street, Barnsley. My grandad will pay you when we get there."

"Are you sure? That's quite a fare."

"Certain."

The taxi driver took pity on them – probably because of Jake's clearly fragile condition. "OK. Get in."

When Grandad came back into the living room, he was making a tutting noise with his tongue. "Twenty-eight pounds! I gave him thirty and he seemed to think it was a tip. Didn't cough up the change too lightly. It was one and three on the bus just a few years back." He pocketed the two pound coins, glanced at Erika and then looked back at Jake. "You've gone a few rounds with a heavyweight. You'd better tell me what's worth twenty-eight pounds of my money, lad."

The painkillers were kicking in. Jake was able to give Grandad a coherent picture of events leading up to the taxi ride out of Sheffield.

"Castleton." The old man shook his head glumly. "I told you, didn't I? You should've had nowt to do with them."

"Yeah, but what do we do now?"

Grandad didn't hesitate. "You stop running round like James Bond. We're going to the hospital to see your mam, of course. The Patmores are good at two things,

Jake. Rushing around being brave isn't one of them. We interpret clouds and we care about other folk."

"Does that mean another taxi?" Erika asked, getting her mobile out. She'd turned it off earlier to avoid being pestered by calls from her mum.

"Put your new-fangled thing away, lass. Patmores look after their money. Twenty-eight pounds! Her next door will give us a lift. She owes me that after I shot all her pigeons for her."

CHAPTER 36

Carly looked like the female version of Frankenstein's monster. She was a patchwork of swellings, bandages and bruises. And she could barely utter a word. But she was alive. She might have even attempted a smile when she saw Jake.

Jake put his head close to his mum's so that he could catch her words.

"That chip."

He looked puzzled for a moment and then he remembered. "The extra one you put in TC?"

His mum nodded feebly once.

"What about it?" he asked.

"You want it."

"All right," Jake said. "I'll find it."

"After . . . when I'm . . ."

"Yes? I'm listening, Mum."

Carly seemed determined to finish her sentence. "When I'm better . . ." Her voice faded away.

"What did she say?" Erika asked.

With a tear in his eye, Jake answered, "When she's better, we're going to talk about Dad."

A nurse ushered them away from Carly's bed, telling them that the patient needed sleep. Visitors and talk could come later.

Outside the ward, Grandad Patmore put his cap back on. "A chip?" He shrugged. "I don't suppose that's something you eat, is it?"

Jake's home was a bombsite. The left-hand side appeared to be untouched but the right – the kitchen and part of the bathroom above – was a mess. At least the walls were intact. The structural damage seemed to be restricted to the windows, doors and roof. The entire place was ringed with tape, warning people not to go any closer.

The police officer standing near the front door watched them for a few seconds and then strolled forward. "This isn't your place by any chance, is it?"

"My grandson's. Jake."

The policeman nodded. "Jake Patmore?"

"Yes," Jake replied.

"I'm sorry. We're going to want to talk to you, but it all looks very straight forward."

"Straight forward?"

"The fire fighters found the gas hob was on."

"Oh? What about the pipe?"

"Pipe? What pipe?" the policeman asked.

"It wasn't an accident," Jake insisted.

"We didn't find any suspicious circumstances."

"I've got to come in," said Jake. "I can show you. I can prove it!"

"Sorry. It's not safe yet. And it's best for you to get over the accident before we interview you. People can come out with all sorts of strange ideas after an accident. It's the shock – people don't know what they're saying sometimes."

So, Castleton people had gone in after the explosion to tighten the nut on the supply and make it look like an accident. A faulty cooker or a scatty owner forgetting to light the hob before gas filled the room. Jake had the awful feeling that they might have taken TC away as well. "But I've got to!" he cried.

Grandad stepped in and said, "Look, I'm sorry about this. He's had a rough time. You'll be wanting my details so you can contact us in a day or two when he's ... you know ... feeling better." He turned to Erika and said, "You take him for a walk. Give the lad some fresh air while I sort this out. All right? Meet me back here. No more than five minutes, mind."

Erika nodded, took Jake's hand and dragged him away. Out of view of the policeman, she stopped. "Hey. Your grandad's a cool operator. He's bought us five minutes. Come on. Can we get into the back garden while he's keeping the law occupied?"

Consumed by his own distress, Jake hadn't realised that Grandad was providing a diversion. "Er ... Yes.

Down next door's drive. You can squeeze through the hedge."

Without a sound, they crept down the passageway between the houses and stopped where the laurels thinned.

"Look!" Erika said, pointing through the leaves.

The lawn had disappeared under a layer of broken tiles, powdered plaster, mangled pieces of the cooker, shredded tea towels, cutlery and broken crockery, part of the kitchen tabletop, glass, and packets of food. It was like something on the news after a not-so-smart missile had hit someone's house. But amidst the fallout, a lifeless metallic dog was sprawled a metre away from one of the kitchen windows.

"There," Jake cried quietly, suddenly cheered by the fact that he might be able to carry out his mum's wishes. "Everyone round here knows about TC. We're famous for having a robot dog. I suppose, if he disappeared, it'd be suspicious."

"And Mum's heavies thought there's no harm leaving him. They didn't know about your mum's chip. What's it do, anyway?"

Jake shrugged. "It kept a list of hardware inside TC. Maybe more." Getting down on all fours, he whispered, "I'm going to get it."

Erika held him back. "Are you well enough? I think I'd better go."

"I know where to look and which flash card it is."

Erika sighed and nodded. "All right. But be careful. Don't let them see you."

Crawling through the hedge, Jake stumbled across part of his weather station straight away. Shaking his head sadly, he looked around. Over to his left, he could just see Grandad talking to the police officer. Once Jake had gone another few metres into the bombsite, he'd be out of their view. Yet he didn't know if there were any police officers or fire fighters watching him from inside. He couldn't afford to worry about it. Going as fast as he could without making too much noise, he scrambled over the debris on hands and knees as jerkily as Tin Can used to walk.

To the right of TC, water was trickling from an overflow pipe or maybe from the exposed bathroom. Ignoring it, Jake went up to the disabled robot. He also had to ignore the pain in his left leg and both arms as he put yet more strain on his injuries. Opening the small panel in Tin Can's left flank, Jake spotted the flash card at once. Breathing a sigh of relief, he grabbed its edge. He was about to remove it when he heard voices above him. He froze.

"You've videoed everything?"

"Yes."

"And Transco are happy the gas supply's OK?"

"They've finished and given us the all-clear."

"Right. We're pretty much done here. I'll get the surveyors and engineers in."

Footsteps retreated.

Looking towards the hedge, Jake could just make out Erika among the laurels. She had her thumb up. Then she beckoned for him to return. Jake plucked out the small chip in its blue plastic casing and slipped it into his trouser pocket. Dog-style, he hurried back across the junk-strewn lawn.

Forcing his aching body through the hedge, he straightened up with a groan.

"All right?" Erika asked.

"Sort of." After seeing his mum, he couldn't complain about his minor injuries.

"You got it?"

In reply, he tapped his pocket.

"Hey, look at you!" Erika muttered. "You're covered in dust. If we go back with you like that . . . bit of a giveaway." She began to brush him down with her hands, especially his trousers and particularly around the knees.

"Ouch!"

"Sorry. Got to be done," she said bossily.

When they rejoined Grandad, Jake didn't look as if he'd benefited from his five minutes of fresh air. He appeared to be worse.

The policeman gazed at him with sympathy and some suspicion.

Grandad said, "Ah. You're back. Good. Apparently, a Mrs Webb has been round – with a photographer – for the local press, but she asked after you as well."

The officer nodded. "Described herself as a friend of the family. Most concerned, she was."

"Yes." Thinking of Aidan's knowledge of computers, Jake added, "Perhaps . . . She's not far away. We ought to go and see her." At Aidan's place, they could examine the contents of the memory card.

On the way, Jake began to flag. He was comforted by Erika's arm around his waist and he leaned more and more against her, but the sheer scale of events was getting the better of him.

"Did you get your chip thing, then?" Grandad asked. Jake nodded.

"Well, I don't understand, but it must be important."

Jake used his last remaining energy to turn towards Grandad and say, "I thought you didn't approve of doing a James Bond. But you cleared the way for us."

Grandad thought about it for a few seconds and then said, "I didn't get involved once before and look what happened to your grandma."

Mrs Webb was in her study writing an article about the local gas explosion and Aidan was listening to his latest mixes. He took one look at Jake and said, "Wow. What a mess!"

Mrs Webb dashed in, saying, "Are you all right, Jake? What happened? How's your mum? Here, sit down."

Exhausted, Jake collapsed onto the settee. "She's . . . not good," he replied. He wasn't up to explaining. He lolled on the couch, recovering, while Grandad Patmore and Erika filled in the story.

When they'd finished, Jake said wearily, "The real reason we're here is this." He leaned to one side and fumbled around in his trouser pocket. His expression changed by degrees from fatigue to bewilderment to panic. Like his dad's letter, the precious chip had gone.

CHAPTER 37

Erika stared back at Jake. "What are you looking at me like that for?"

Aidan gazed at her accusingly as well. His expression suggested he knew exactly what Jake was thinking.

Grandad Patmore and Mrs Webb stood there in silence, realising that they were witnessing a crucial moment between three friends but remaining totally mystified by it.

Jake's trust and affection for Erika had disappeared in a flash. He remembered how Erika had brushed his trousers, how she'd put her arm around him, how her hand had rested on his hip just above the pocket where he'd stashed the chip. And there was her pedigree. Jake wondered what she had inherited from the woman who had stolen his dad's letter. "You . . ." He hesitated. He couldn't bring himself to denounce her aloud.

"If it's gone, don't blame me!" she blurted out. "I didn't nick it. I'm risking everything to help you, you know. I'm here, aren't I? Not with Mum. I'm not like her. What's going to happen to me when she finds out what I'm up to? My life goes up in smoke, that's what. And it's all for you!" Furiously, she folded her arms and turned her back on the boys.

Mrs Webb interceded. "Look . . . er . . . before we all get too heated, can I suggest you look between the cushions, Jake? That's where most things in this house end up. Money, keys, the lot."

Jake shuffled along the sofa so that Aidan could get his hand into the gap near Jake's pocket. He rummaged around for a few seconds and then fished out a Biro and a small blue mobile disk. Holding out the chip on his open palm, Aidan said, "Got it."

Jake didn't know whether to feel relieved or embarrassed. "Sorry, Erika," he said. "I shouldn't . . ."

But Erika wasn't going to listen. She charged towards the door. Before she left, she hesitated and said, "That's twice you've blamed me for something. Passing secrets to Mum and now this. There's too much screwy stuff between you and Mum. You'll never trust me, not totally."

"Erika!" Jake tried to get to his feet but, groaning with pain, fell back onto the sofa.

The slamming of the door was Erika's only response. "No! please, I . . ."

Mrs Webb touched his shoulder. "She's gone, Jake. She needs some space. She'll be back."

Jake wasn't so sure. He hung his head in his hands.

*

Half an hour later, Aidan was sitting in front of the monitor while the other three looked over his shoulder. The catalogue of TC's hardware was no longer stored in the chip. Instead, it provided a list of the devices that it had detected on the Webbs' computer. But there was one new and very large file in the memory card that hadn't been there before. Aidan double-clicked on it.

"It's . . . er . . . It's in some strange language I don't know," he said, screwing up his face as he looked at the first page of symbols, numbers and words. "But I've seen this sort of thing before. It's some sort of machine code – sets of commands."

Grandad gave up. He went to the window and gazed out at the early-evening sky where two aeroplanes were circling.

Hanging onto the back of Aidan's seat, Jake nodded. "I bet I know what it is. The chip's captured all TC's instructions. Scroll down a few pages, Aidan. See if it says where they came from."

It was an unintelligible document.

Frustrated, Aidan said, "We need your mum to translate."

"True, but . . ." Grunting at a twinge of pain, Jake leaned over Aidan's shoulder and pointed at a line in the middle part of the screen.

CC NRR: Incoming command file.

285

"CC. Castleton Computing," said Aidan.

"I don't know what the middle R's for," Jake added, "but it's Neisha R Ray."

Aidan swivelled in his seat, a look of triumph on his face. "This is saying Tin Can was taking orders from Erika's mum!"

"Yes," Jake replied. "And an expert – like Mum – will be able to read what the orders were."

"Got 'em!" Aidan cried. "Easy-peasy."

Jake nodded. He was too tired, too tender, too worried about his mum and too upset about Erika to celebrate. He couldn't celebrate until he'd made amends with Erika, until he'd told her how stupid he'd been. And he was wondering where she'd gone. He was hoping she was safe from her own mother.

Mrs Webb interrupted again. "Before you get carried away, copy the file, Aidan. If it's that important, you don't want all your eggs in one basket."

For once, Aidan couldn't criticise his mother. He even congratulated her. "Good point. I'll put it on a CD – and another memory card, just in case." He got down on his knees so he could reach round to the USB port at the back of the processor.

Grimacing, Grandad Patmore looked across at his grandson and said, "Jake. Come here, lad. Tell me if you've ever seen owt like this."

"What?" Jake staggered to the window and followed his Grandad's eyes upwards.

"It's not natural," Grandad muttered, his voice quivering.

A huge billowing cloud was forming as quickly as smoke gushing from an industrial chimney. It was spreading menacingly outwards and aloft, obliterating the clear sky.

Jake had heard the drone of aircraft but he hadn't thought of it as anything other than innocent flights overhead. Now, watching the ragged cloud getting thicker and darker by the second, he realised that he was wrong. "They've seeded something up there!" he exclaimed.

"Seeded? You mean . . ."

"Yes. It's Castleton!" Jake shouted at Aidan, "Quick. We've got to get out of here. Get a copy and let's go."

"I'm rebooting so the computer sees the memory card."

"Hurry."

"Did Erika tell them we're here?" Aidan said.

Jake shook his head firmly. "Not a chance. She wouldn't. I'm sure. I bet Neisha guessed we'd turn up at my place or here sooner or later. She probably had people watching out for us."

Aidan turned his attention back to the PC that had just finished reloading.

Outside, the deep grey cloud was drifting closer and closer on the breeze.

"You go," Aidan said. "I'll finish here and catch you up."

Jake didn't wait for Mrs Webb or Grandad to reply. "No. We stick together."

All four of them turned towards the window as hail began to hammer on the glass.

Mrs Webb asked, "Are we safe in here?"

"If it comes to lightning, a house is about the safest place to be. Away from doors and windows." Grandad stepped back and glanced at Aidan. "And away from anything electrical."

Jake knew that many people had been struck in their homes by an electrical bolt coming down the phone line during a call. Sometimes, the receiver melted and welded itself to the side of the victim's face. Lightning also hijacked TVs, radios and computers to get at anyone sheltering in a house.

"Nearly done," Aidan yelled above the clatter of the thunderstorm.

Jake looked at the outside, transformed from a tranquil evening into a tempest, from day into night. Through the hail and darkness, he saw Mrs Webb's car parked beside a lamppost. Looking at her, he said, "Castleton's targeting this house. The best place to be is somewhere else. Or in a car."

To check that Jake knew his facts, she glanced at Grandad Patmore.

He nodded. "They say lightning goes down the outside of a car, not through it."

"We'll make a run for it, then."

Aidan reached round to the back of the consul and pulled out the original flash card and his copy. "Ready." Tapping his pocket, he said, "I've got it on CD as well."

"Coat on," Mrs Webb shouted at him.

"No," Jake said. "No time. We've just got to go."

Mrs Webb unlocked the car doors remotely from the porch and then went first. The other three followed in a line. As they dashed down the short garden path, it was like being pelted with pebbles. Above them, the air crackled with electricity.

Mrs Webb was half in the car and half out when the lightning came. The others were clustered around the gate. All of them came to an abrupt involuntary halt. The underside of the artificial cumulonimbus came to life, shooting a bolt of lightning at them. Frying the air, the sudden streak discharged itself on the street-light. The electricity ran to ground, instantly boiling the rain and hail on the lamppost, shrouding it with steam.

Mrs Webb was thrown from the car and landed on the white line in the middle of the road. Aidan was flung onto the lawn where he lay on a bed of hailstones. Grandad's cap flew from his head and his remaining hair stood on end.

Thunder hit them immediately. The shockwave blasted their eardrums and the vibration passed right through them, rattling every organ.

Grandad was stunned, unable to move. The fierce flash had dazzled him.

Jake tried to shut out the intense buzzing inside his head, the ringing in his ears, and the churning of his stomach. He grabbed the old man's arm and guided him to the car door. Grandad's hand went to his head as if his greatest loss was his cap.

Unnerved and confused, Aidan got to his feet, fell over again and then part-crawled, part-staggered to the gate. He yanked himself upright, lurched across the pavement and tumbled into the back of the car. His mum, made for the driver's seat again, ignoring the grazes on her palms and legs.

The four car doors slammed shut.

Mrs Webb struggled to get the key in the ignition because her hands were trembling so much. When she finally started the engine, she realised that she couldn't see a thing out of the windscreen. A curtain of white reduced visibility almost to zero. She set the wipers to their highest speed and turned on her headlights. Twisting in her seat, she looked at Jake and shrugged hopelessly.

"We've got to go!" he shouted above the pounding on the roof.

Mrs Webb leaned forward, squinting into the gloom, the rain and hail. The car jolted and bumped down from the kerb.

Behind them, there was a second flash and crash.

None of them saw what happened but, this time, the malicious streak of electricity hit the Webbs' TV aerial. The power surged down the cable and disintegrated the television. A shower of sparks, glass and electronic components filled the living room and the smoke alarm began to howl.

Catching the second strike in her rear-view mirror, Mrs Webb accelerated as best she could and shifted clumsily through the gears. At twenty miles an hour, the car seemed to be travelling far too fast for the conditions. Coming to the end of the street, she braked and yelled, "Where are we going?"

They all looked at Jake.

The first white flash of lightning seemed to be imprinted on Jake's eye. He could still see it when he blinked. "Er . . . Grandad's," he replied. "Barnsley. Castleton don't know about that."

Mrs Webb pulled out from the junction, assuming that no one else would be stupid enough to drive through this weather. After a hundred blind metres, her headlights began to pick out the road. The clatter on the roof eased as the hail turned to rain. She put her foot down and headed for safe haven in Barnsley.

CHAPTER 38

Jake had never felt so nervous in his life as he waited in the familiar reception. The muscles in his neck were locked and tension hammered at his head. His breath came in short shallow gasps. In his pocket, the memory card burned.

The woman on the desk announced, "You can go in now. You know where it is, don't you?"

Jake nodded. He got up and shuffled slowly towards Gordon Dell's office.

As soon as he opened the door and slipped inside, Gordon said, "We heard about your accident. How's Carly – your mum?" A breathtaking impression of concern was written on his face.

Jake did not reply. He kept to the lines he'd rehearsed. "I've come for my dad's letter."

Behind the large desk, Gordon appeared to be bewildered. "Letter? Sorry? What letter?"

Jake took the flash card out of his pocket and tossed it in front of the Head of Castleton Computing.

Gordon looked down at the morsel on his desk and said, "What's this?"

"Plug it into your computer and have a look. It's what you get in return for the letter."

Gordon looked at Brian and then nodded towards the mobile disk.

Brian took it and pushed it into the computer's USB port.

Neisha stood silently at the back of the room by the window. She had not dared to make eye contact with Jake.

"You didn't give us the latest on your mum," Gordon said.

"She's alive," Jake answered tersely.

"Yes. We called the hospital. We sent her a small token of our best wishes."

His mum had refused their showy bouquet of flowers. "She gave it to an old woman who didn't have any."

"As long as someone gets the bene—"

Brian interrupted, saying, "You'd better look at this." He glanced uncomfortably towards Neisha.

"What is it?" Gordon asked, leaning forward to inspect the screen.

Behind the two men, Neisha had turned as white as newly formed snow.

"It's a complete set of instructions transmitted from here to one of our robots," Brian replied. "Tin Can, to be exact. It's dated and named. It came from Neisha."

Briefly, Gordon looked up at Jake.

Jake hoped that he'd spotted a flash of shame in Gordon's expression, but it was probably only guilt.

"Does it describe exactly what the robot was programmed to do?"

Brian didn't answer at once. He scrolled down the screen, skimming over the countless lines of code. "Yes. It looks like it."

"I see." Addressing Jake again, Gordon asked, "Why have you brought it in?"

"I thought you'd want it back."

"In return for a letter?"

"Yes."

Gordon sat back in his chair as if trying to give the impression that he was unconcerned. "Is that what all this is about? An old letter."

Jake nodded, his heart pounding.

Gordon sighed and opened one of his drawers. He poked around inside for a few seconds, closed it, and then delved into a different drawer. Eventually, he found the five pages of untidy handwriting and held them out towards Jake. "I was going to get rid of this, but I forgot all about it."

"That tells me exactly what you thought of him," Jake said as he took it back. "You're not fit to even touch it. And you had no right to." Once again, the letter belonged to Jake and Jake alone. He experienced a warmth spreading from his hand to the rest of his body. Perhaps it was a feeling of confidence and control.

"We're not fools in here, are we, Jake? Neither are you." Gordon waved towards the monitor. "Am I right in thinking this isn't the only copy of the robot's activities?"

Jake nodded again.

"What are you going to do with it?"

Jake had wondered if he should trade the other copies for the disarming of the satellites and the deletion of the weather model, but he decided that it was too chancy. He could never be certain that they'd terminated the satellites because he couldn't see their destruction with his own eyes. And there could always be a hidden copy of the weather software. He'd decided it was time to step aside. It was time to stop running round like James Bond. "The press have got one and the police are looking at another right now." The file would feed the coming media frenzy and it would form the centrepiece in a case of attempted murder.

With a sideways glance at Neisha, Gordon said, "I have to tell you. I'm not responsible – and the company can't be responsible – for everything every employee does."

Finally, Neisha piped up. "No, Gordon. You're not going to lay it all on me. You knew exactly what I was doing. I was only doing what you—"

Gordon laughed. "That's not true."

Neisha hesitated and took a deep breath. "You know,

nine years ago, when you first told me to do something about Craig, I wondered if it'd ever turn out like this. Me in deep trouble and you pure as a newborn baby. Well, I've got news for you. You're right, I'm not a fool. I got myself an insurance policy."

"What do you mean?" At last, Gordon Dell looked uneasy.

"We had a telephone conversation about Craig Patmore. Back then, we couldn't conjure up our own weather. You talked about using Carly's prototype to surprise him when he went out chasing storms."

Gordon shook his head. "I don't recall anything like that. You're making—"

Neisha's affected laugh sounded a little hysterical. "There were no flash cards in those days, but we could tape phone calls on cassettes. Remember them? Old technology, not great quality, but they worked. I've got an old but perfectly preserved recording."

Jake looked at the three of them in disdain. Happy to let them self-destruct in private, he walked away without another word.

CHAPTER 39

By the time that Jake's mum left hospital, she didn't have to worry about getting by without Castleton Computing. Jake had already spoken to Timo Scarpa. "His insurance company'll pay me lots. Nothing to do with changing the weather," Jake added hastily. "Just to forecast and warn him what's coming. And that's not all. He contacted a few people about me. You're not going to believe this, but a motor racing team and a couple of airports are testing me out. And I'm a weather consultant for the NHS."

"What? The NHS?"

"It's all about predicting when old folk are going to slip over and break their hips because it's wet or icy. In summer, it's forecasting hot spells that bring on breathing difficulties and heat exhaustion. Easy. They want advance warning of what sort of beds, equipment and staff they're going to need. And the Met Office in Exeter's interested . . ."

"Slow down!" said Carly. "You're giving me a headache."

"Anyway, you don't have to worry about money."

"I'm just supposed to live off my son, eh?"

"You can get a job – when you're up to it."

Carly smiled. "That's good of you. Thanks." She looked into Jake's face and said, "You're forgetting about school."

"No. It doesn't take me long to predict the weather. I can fit it in around school. Evenings, Saturdays, holidays. Henson's promising me a job next year – when I'm sixteen – and a great big pay packet."

Bewildered, Carly shook her head. "We'll talk about it later. For now, there's so much I've got to catch up on. Is Aidan OK – and his mum?"

"Fine. Their house got roughed up but it was insured by Henson. New telly, new windows, new front room, and they'll be sitting pretty. It's worked out well for Mrs Webb. After her exclusives in the local rag, she's been snapped up by one of the big, national papers."

Carly nodded. Anxiously, she asked, "When they took Neisha away, what happened to Erika?"

"She went to live with her father."

"Will you keep in touch? Does he live around here?"

"New Zealand."

"Ah. Now you mention it, Neisha told me that ages ago. It's . . . a long way. Sorry, Jake."

Jake paused before he replied. "It wouldn't have worked out. Not really. I guess it was a trust thing. I think I hurt her too much by doubting her – twice. And her mum'll always be there – banged up, I know – but she'd be a constant reminder. Tricky for both of us. No, it's best . . ." He closed his eyes and attempted a casual shrug, but he failed to disguise the hurt that he felt.

Carly reached out and squeezed his arm. She couldn't say anything to make it better.

It was a time of rebuilding. When Jake had broken the kitchen window and let out a lot of gas, he'd lessened the force of the explosion and limited the damage. The basic structure of the house was still sound. The roof, windows, doors and utilities had been replaced and the redecoration was well underway. But it wasn't just their home. Carly and Jake were rebuilding their lives.

Kneeling on the floor of the living room, Carly was going through the untidy heaps of things that the fire team had salvaged from the fallout. She picked up and put aside two dishevelled cookbooks. "This is just so much junk now." The next item was a saucer. She laughed. "I don't know how this survived," she said, "but there's only one and no cups left to go with it. Not much you can do with one saucer and no cup. And I haven't got a single wine glass left."

Jake looked at his mum and recalled how much she used to drink. "Good," he replied.

Smiling, Carly said, "Yes. I can take a hint." She moved the saucer onto the growing pile of rubbish and immediately froze.

Looking down at her, Jake said, "What's up?"

Her look of shock was evolving into surprise. "I didn't know . . . I threw out so much when your dad died. I wonder where this has been hiding. I'd completely forgotten about it."

Jake joined her on the carpet. "What?"

"An old photo."

"Yeah, but what is it?"

Jake looked at it from two different angles until he worked it out. He was looking at a man's chin, shoulder and part of his arm from a crazy perspective. Puzzled, Jake turned to his mum.

"Don't you recognise it?" Now, there was the beginning of another smile on her face.

"No. Should I?"

"In a way, yes. It's your dad." She grasped her walking stick and dragged herself upright. "It's the first picture you ever took. And the last one you took of your dad."

"But . . . How come?"

Carly plonked herself down into an easy chair with a muted groan. "He was so proud of you. He was getting up close to take a photo of you but you were into everything. You were . . . I don't know . . . a toddler at the time. Your eyes used to follow him everywhere, watching everything he did. You reached up and grabbed the camera. Your dad almost dropped it, you almost caught it, and your finger hit the button. And there you are," she said, nodding at the bizarre photograph in Jake's hand, "your first masterpiece: close-up of a weather prophet."

Jake swallowed twice, trying not to cry over a shabby, stupid, distorted photo. "Can I keep it?" he asked.

"It's yours."

At once, he flew upstairs to his bedroom and looked around the wall for a bit of free space. He slotted the tattered photograph of his dad between an on-rushing tornado and a wistful Erika in the park.

CHAPTER 40

If Gordon Dell and Neisha Ray had not bickered so much – each accusing the other of responsibility for the deaths of Craig Patmore and Robert Goodhart – the police would not have been able to add murder to the long list of their offences.

By the end of the investigation, the case against Brian Mosby was flimsy, even though he was a vital part of the company that would be convicted of corporate manslaughter for creating the fatal Brazilian storm. As an individual, Mosby was not charged. His solicitor argued successfully that he had simply carried out the terms of his employment. If there was a crime, it lay with the manager who gave him his duties.

So, Brian Mosby was a free man, looking for a fresh start. He found it when he was appointed to the post of lecturer in Atmospheric and Environmental Sciences at the University of Oklahoma, USA. He uprooted himself from Sheffield and he headed for Norman, Oklahoma, with a biometric passport, a visa and the remnants of his old life in packing cases. He would pursue his research into extreme weather where he could see it close up – in the heart of Tornado Alley.

As soon as he touched down in the American Midwest, though, he ran into American bureaucracy and security. The customs officials in Immigration gave him a hard time. They took his fingerprints, photographed him, and quizzed him about his reasons for entering the country. They scrutinised every piece of paperwork to prove that he was who he said he was and that his job was genuine rather than the product of a fanciful imagination or a cover for some hostile un-American activity. And, when they'd finished with his paperwork and passport, they searched his hand luggage thoroughly, piece by piece, as if they had all the time in the world.

When the first customs officer drew a set of twenty-five CDs out of his bag, she raised her eyebrows questioningly.

"They're to do with work," Brian explained. "Just meteorological data and that sort of thing." After all, he'd taken Craig Patmore's weather model under his wing once before. He intended to do it again in his new life. He would feed his need for power over the weather by saving people from a cruel atmosphere. He'd be his own boss this time and he would not be seduced by its military potential.

The officer said, "We're going to confiscate them."

"You can't!" Brian uttered.

Both of the officials laughed at him. "We can. We can do whatever we want if we think there's a chance something could jeopardise national security."

"My CDs? They're for weather forecasting."

"Fine. In that case, when we have them examined, there'll be no issues and you'll get them back."

"But—"

"Look," said the second officer. "For all we know, they could be instructions for making bombs, blueprints of aircraft, hijack plans, or schematics of sensitive sites. You get the picture? We don't take chances any more."

"But they're not. They're harmless. And I'm not a terrorist."

A large and rugged man came up behind the two staff and stood between them. His uniformed chest was decorated with a fearsome collection of medals. He spoke in a deep and severe southern drawl. It was the sort of voice that no one questioned. "My colleagues are right to insist." He held out his hand and at once the first officer placed the compact disks on his palm. He looked directly into Brian's face and said, "Thank you, sir."

Open-mouthed, Brian watched the military man walk away with his future. "But . . ."

"You're finished in Immigration. You can pack and proceed."

"Who was that?" Brian muttered to the customs official.

"That," she answered, "was Colonel Emery B Husband Jr. of the US Air Force. Not a man to be crossed."

ABOUT THE AUTHOR

Malcolm Rose was born in England during the devastating gale of 31st January and 1st February 1953. The storm caused severe coastal flooding and killed over 530 people in Britain and 1,836 in the Netherlands. It was Britain's worst peacetime disaster of the 20th century.

Malcolm began writing stories as a hobby while taking a PhD in Chemistry at York University. Until 1996, he was a Lecturer in Chemistry at the Open University. This job left very little time for writing fiction, which he did mostly after midnight. Perhaps that's why he writes many strong scenes set on dark nights! Having put aside his test-tubes and picked up a pen, he is now a full-time writer, living in Sheffield.

He writes mainly thrillers and crime stories, enjoying himself most when the story has a basis in modern science. Most of his crime stories are awash with the gruesome bits of forensic science. His thrillers are frequently fuelled by chemistry, biology and, in the case of

Hurricane Force, meteorology. Because science is always advancing, it provides an endless source of ideas for a novelist. Malcolm has won the Angus Book Award (twice) and the Lancashire Children's Book of the Year Award.

Find out more at www.malcolmrose.co.uk

SO BELOW BY MATT WHYMAN

If you're ever in great danger, with nowhere else to turn, maybe you'll find help in the world beneath your feet.

That's what happens to Yoshi, one night in London's Chinatown. Fleeing from a mysterious pursuer, the boy finds himself in a sprawling, subterranean network of tunnels, tracks, vaults and lost waterways. It's also home to a band of urchins schooled in modern magic – the art of illusion and trickery.

Aided by his new friends, Yoshi uncovers his own vital part in a mission to tap into ancient forces underpinning the capital. But can he pull off the performance of a lifetime before his past catches up with him, or will life on street level fall under a dark and dangerous spell?

Introducing a gripping urban fantasy for all ages, from the acclaimed author of *Boy Kills Man*. No wizards, no dragons . . . and no way you'll view city-life through the same eyes again.

ISBN: 0-689-87264-X

TO BE A NINJA BY BENEDICT JACKA

Ignis and Allandra are on the run. Escaping from the clutches of their drug baron father, they have managed to find sanctuary deep in the forest, while Allandra's twin, Michael, has been re-captured. Their new home: Rokkaku, a secret training school for ninjas.

For the rebellious Ignis, stumbling upon the hidden school is the last thing he wants – replacing one set of rules and regulations with another. For Allandra, it offers the perfect hiding place, and a chance to make true friends at last. But each day is a struggle: avoiding discovery, bowing to rules, dealing with bullies and going through rigorous training. Finally Allandra sets off to rescue her twin – but can she save Michael, without sacrificing herself?

ISBN: 1-416-90128-0

OUTCAST • WURM WAR
Christopher Golden and Thomas E. Sniegoski

TIMOTHY CADE is the only boy in the world without magical powers – and everyone wants him . . . dead or alive!

TIMOTHY AND CASSANDRA may have beaten the evil sorcerer Alhazred, but their problems are far from over. Alhazred was connected so closely to the matrix energy that his death caused a magical blow-out, dimming all the sorcerous power, both in people and in lights. The blow-out has also weakened the dimensional barrier that keeps the Wurm out of Arcanum. Now, for the first time in decades, the Wurm have the chance to wreak their vengeance upon the mages who sought to destroy them. Can Timothy and Cassandra end the feud before the Wurm devastate Arcanum?

ISBN: 0-689-87304-2

PENDRAGON · RIVERS OF ZADAA
D. J. MACHALE

Bobby's adventure continues as he tries to save all of Halla from destruction. This time he's off to the land of Zadaa, where the traveller, Loor, lives. Saint Dane is set to instigate trouble between the two tribes that live here – the Batu and the Rokador.

They are on the brink of a civil war, and Saint Dane is planning to give them the final push – unless Bobby Pendragon can stop him . . .

ISBN: 0-689-87553-3

VAMPIRATES • DEMONS OF THE OCEAN
JUSTIN SOMPER

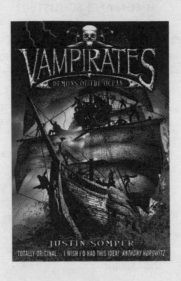

The year is 2505. The oceans have risen. A new era of piracy is dawning. A vicious storm separates twins Connor and Grace Tempest, destroying their boat and leaving them fighting for their lives in the cruel, cold water.

Picked up by one of the more notorious pirate ships, Connor soon finds himself wielding a cutlass. But does he have the stomach to be a pirate?

Grace finds herself aboard a more mysterious ship. Kept under lock and key, she's assured no harm will come to her, just as long as she follows the enigmatic captain's rules . . .

Can the twins survive life on-board – and find their way back to each other? Join them as they journey into uncharted waters. The voyage of the vampirates is about to begin . . .

ISBN: 0-689-87263-1